HI

KEN GREENHALL was b... grants from England. ... 15, worked at a record st... military, serving in Germ... State University and moved to New York, where he worked as an editor of reference books, first on the staff of the *Encyclopedia Americana* and later for the *New Columbia Encyclopedia*. Greenhall had a longtime interest in the supernatural and took leave from his job to write his first novel, *Elizabeth* (1976), a tale of witchcraft published under his mother's maiden name, Jessica Hamilton. Several more novels followed, including *Hell Hound* (1977), which was published abroad as *Baxter* and adapted for a critically acclaimed 1989 French film under that title. Greenhall died in 2014.

By Ken Greenhall

Elizabeth (1976)*
Hell Hound (1977)*
Childgrave (1982)*
The Companion (1988)
Deathchain (1991)
Lenoir (1998)

HELL HOUND

BY KEN GREENHALL

WITH A NEW INTRODUCTION BY
GRADY HENDRIX

VALANCOURT BOOKS

Hell Hound by Ken Greenhall
First published by Zebra Books in 1977
First Valancourt Books edition published 2017
Special Paperbacks from Hell edition published 2023
Reprinted from the British edition published by Harrap in 1977

Published by Valancourt Books, Richmond, Virginia
http://www.valancourtbooks.com

ISBN 978-1-954321-83-0 (trade paperback)
Also available as an electronic book and an audiobook.

Cover restoration and design by M. S. Corley
Set in Dante MT

INTRODUCTION

I need to introduce you to Ken Greenhall because a) he's dead and can't introduce himself, and b) few authors have been so completely erased. His six novels are out of print. He has no Wikipedia page, there's barely any bibliographic reference, and the handful of online mentions he rates can't even agree on whether he's a man or a woman. Is Greenhall the author and Jessica Hamilton the pseudonym? Or is Hamilton the writer and Greenhall her creation?

Greenhall's literary light isn't guttering, it's extinguished. His entire output survives as a handful of faded mass market paperbacks found on musty swap shop shelves, passed between true believers, occasionally sold online for a penny plus shipping. He is horror fiction's invisible man. He is also one of its greatest stylists.

> 'When I was younger I saw James, my father's brother, look from our dog to me without changing his expression. I soon taught him to look at me in a way he looked at nothing else.'   —*Elizabeth* (written as Jessica Hamilton)

> 'There was a time when my life was like yours. I ate veal occasionally, and avoided people who had a serious interest in God. I smiled at clients during the day, disappearing beneath the black velvet hood from time to time to steal their souls.'   —*Childgrave*

> 'They are deranged. They are pale, their country is flat and wet, and they have no souls. I believe they are being punished for having only one god.'   —*Lenoir*

The blockbuster successes of *Rosemary's Baby*, *The Exorcist*, and *The Other* between 1968 and 1971 launched a publishing gold rush, carpeting bookstores with paperbacks embossed with foil, eye-melting cover art, and tabloid titles: *Satan's Love Child*, *Queen of Hell*, *The Desecration of Susan Browning*. The rush lasted into the early Nineties when a combination of too many cheap books, too many collapsing imprints, and publishing house merger mania popped the bubble and horror died like a dog.

In the midst of these roaring white water rapids, Greenhall was hard to hear. When other authors shouted, he whispered. Where other authors reached for the grotesque, he strove for understatement. The most popular books of the day were bulging slabs of wood pulp dripping with shock effects. Greenhall's books were precise and trim. They didn't gross you out, or send you reeling, or destroy your mind, they simply and methodically unstrung your nerves. He didn't aim to terrify, he wanted to undermine your sense of comfort. It's a harder trick, but it lasts longer.

Born in Detroit in 1928 to parents who had just emigrated from the United Kingdom, Ken Greenhall graduated from high school at the age of 15 and went to work in his father's record store until he joined the army and was stationed in Germany. On his return, he moved to New York City and got a job editing the *Encyclopedia Americana* and the *Columbia Encyclopedia*. He'd stay on their staff for the rest of his working life. In 1977, he married his second wife, Agnes, and decided to write a book, just to see if he could.

Standing 6'3", with strawberry blond hair, Greenhall was driven by challenges. Lots of people play jazz trumpet and love Charlie Parker. Few of them go on to build a harpsichord by hand and teach themselves how to play. When Greenhall got a Rubik's Cube for Christmas he refused to sleep until he solved it, which took him until 5 a.m. that same day. Writing was another challenge for Greenhall, something he did in longhand after work, another puzzle-solving exercise, this one aimed at understanding the mysteries of the human mind.

Voices seduced Greenhall, and every book he wrote was an attempt to see the world through alien eyes. Told from the point of view of a fourteen-year-old girl who believes she's the descendant of a witch, *Elizabeth* is delivered in the clipped, passionless tones of the truly insane. Greenhall's agent, Oscar Collier, sold it quickly and, for reasons no one remembers, it was published under Greenhall's mother's maiden name, Jessica Hamilton.

Fascinated by a sinister-looking Bull Terrier, Greenhall almost immediately set to work on *Hell Hound*, this time determined to see the world through animal eyes. 'The ways they deceive themselves are endless,' Baxter, the titular canine says, and our familiar world seen through his pale blue eyes becomes bizarre, unlinked from emotion or context. Babies are defective because they're helpless ('The child is not normal . . . they feel guilt for having produced it'), the human body is a disadvantage ('The only admirable part of the human body, I think, is the hand'), and self-restraint is the same as self-deception.

Every sentence is a tab of lysergic wordplay as Baxter forces us to see things we consider good—the elderly, people who love their pets, childbirth—as pitiable. But Baxter's is only one of the multiple points of view on display. Mrs. Prescott, the woman who is his first victim, Carl, the 13-year-old Nazi who adopts him, Mr. Best, the next door neighbor who is barely glimpsed, each of them obligingly opens their skulls to share their thoughts. Greenhall doesn't show us how they present themselves to the world, or how they want to be seen, instead he shows us their unvarnished innermost selves, completely free of vanity. The book feels like a machine gun aimed at polite society, unleashed in short, sharp declarative sentences and brisk chapters that fly like bullets.

Hell Hound (or *Baxter*, as it was called when director Jérôme Boivin released his acclaimed French film adaptation in 1989) was to be Greenhall's favorite of his books (besides *Lenoir*). Despite coming onto the market at the peak of the killer animal trend (*Jaws* and *The Rats* in 1974, and a million imitators until *Cujo* in 1981) every single publisher rejected it until it wound up at Zebra Books, a bottom of the barrel paperback publisher who slapped a cheaper-than-usual cover on an even-cheaper paperback and tossed it out onto shelves. The cover art appalled Greenhall, but nobody cared.

After the darkness of *Elizabeth* and *Hell Hound*, Greenhall wanted to write something lighter. Inspired by a photograph of R.D. Laing's four-year-old daughter, he wrote *Childgrave*, about a photographer who seems to be taking pictures of spirits. Written almost entirely in the middle of the night, it's not quite the breath of fresh air Greenhall intended, as it explores the fact that, as one character puts it, 'Maybe God is not civilized.'

Next came *The Companion* about a serial killing angel of mercy who is a paid companion to the elderly, then *Deathchain*, a trifle that feels like the beginning of a series about a dissolute cognac salesman who becomes, in the most accidental way possible, an amateur sleuth. It's not his best work, but even so it's still swift and sure-footed, full of the deft observations and a deceptive simplicity that had become Greenhall's style.

After he retired, Greenhall decided to write the book he'd been pondering for years. *Lenoir* is the story of a black slave in 17th-century Amsterdam who winds up modeling for the Rubens painting, *Four Studies of the Head of a Negro*. Instead of trying to hide his blackness, Lenoir is convinced that it makes him the most handsome man in the Netherlands. He is not the freak, it's the pale people around him who are the outsiders, and he pities and patronizes them in a breathtaking reversal of expectations. *Lenoir* is very close to a masterpiece. It also killed Ken Greenhall's career.

By the time he started to write *Lenoir*, Greenhall had been abandoned by his agent. He went looking for new representation, but was told again and again that he was too old. The research for his book was intense, and writing it consumed him. When he was finished he sold it directly to a small publisher, Zoland Books, best known for its literary fiction. He was 70 and he was exhausted, but happy. *Lenoir* received favorable reviews in the trade publications, *Publisher's Weekly* and *Kirkus*, but Michael Pye, another writer, weighed in for the *New York Times*.

Needlessly snarky, picking irrelevant nits, Pye ignored the impressive act of historical ventriloquism Greenhall accomplished to carp over whether Greenhall accurately depicted the speed of the 17th-century mail service, and whether a song Lenoir sings was anachronistic. Cruel and snide, the review cut Greenhall like a knife. He never wrote again. He died sixteen years later in 2014.

But a book is a life an author leaves us. The reprint of *Hell Hound* that you hold in your hands is a part of Ken Greenhall, and as long as a writer has readers he can never truly die. Greenhall's books have slept for decades, resting beneath the dirt, longing to burst forth and bloom again, waiting for a pair of new eyes. Waiting for you.

GRADY HENDRIX

Grady Hendrix is the *New York Times*-bestselling author of *How to Sell a Haunted House* (out January 2023), *The Final Girl Support Group*, *The Southern Book Club's Guide to Slaying Vampires*, *My Best Friend's Exorcism*, and many more. His history of the horror paperback boom of the '70s and '80s, *Paperbacks from Hell*, won the Stoker Award, and his latest nonfiction book, *These Fists Break Bricks*, is a heavily illustrated history of the kung fu boom in America during the '70s and '80s. You can learn more useless facts about him at www.gradyhendrix.com

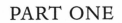

PART ONE

One

Each afternoon as I lie amid the odors of dryness and age I begin to think of the couple, and my excitement grows. I feel the warm patch of sunlight move slowly over my body. My legs twitch, and the delicate hairs in my ears begin to bristle. Soon, from among the gentle sounds of the late summer day, I'll hear the approach of their automobile.

I concentrate on the sporadic drone of distant traffic. One of those sounds will suddenly become distinctive and unmistakable. At that instant I will be fully awake. I will run to the window, push aside the limp, dusty curtains, and wait for the couple to appear.

I have been close to them only once. The woman's foot was bare, and she touched my head. Her scent was exquisite; a subtle blend dominated by an acrid aroma related somehow to sexual readiness. I have seldom known such pleasure.

The sound of their automobile dominates all others now, and in a moment I shall be able to see them. The man maneuvers the car unerringly into the driveway, and for a moment there is life in the neighborhood. Curtains part in other windows, revealing old, resentful faces.

Soon the neighborhood is quiet again, but I stay at the window, staring at the couple's tall, neglected house. What are they doing? How do they live? If I stand rigidly and give their house all my attention I can hear the woman's voice occasionally. But that is not enough. I want to be in their house. I want to be close enough to hear the hiss of fabric against skin as they remove their clothes. I want to put my nose against those discarded garments and distinguish the faint traces of fear and pleasure left by their bodies.

Instead I wait for the old person. She will be home soon, exhausted and uninteresting. She will carry a small package of unpalatable, stale-smelling meat, which she will make even less appealing by frying it in bland grease. Later she will dial the telephone and murmur endlessly into the mouthpiece, pausing occasionally as a tiny, equally weary voice murmurs back at her. It is one of her most puzzling activities. Then, even more strangely, she will turn on the television set and sit staring as it flashes and squeals.

She will invite me to sit with her, and she will stroke my body. Her hand is dry and virtually odorless in itself, smelling only of the things she has touched. After a few minutes I find her unbearable, and I go to the window. Across the dark street I see shadows move past the windows of the couple's house. I hear their laughter.

There is never laughter in this house; only the dull sounds of age and weakness. But I am not weak. I have a strength and resourcefulness that the old woman probably never had.

What are the possibilities of my strength? That is a thought I have never had before. What if some morning as the old woman stood at the head of the staircase she were suddenly to feel a weight thrusting against the back of her legs? What if she were to lunge forward, grasping at the air, striking her thin skull against the edge of a stair? What would become of me if she were found unmoving at the bottom of the stairway?

Someone else would love me, as she has loved me. I'm certain of that. People have a great interest in love. They see it everywhere; probably even in me.

2

There's such love in him, thought Mrs. Prescott. He'll be waiting impatiently in the window, his strange head pushing between the curtains.

She had not been convinced of that love immediately. She had lived for sixty-three years without a pet. And then, six months ago, her daughter had come to visit and presented her with Baxter. Mrs. Prescott recalled the panic she felt when her daughter drove off, leaving her alone with the dog for the first time.

Such an unlikely looking animal. A bull terrier, her daughter had said: a recognized breed. Why would anyone want to perpetuate such ugliness? A head like a hatchet. Malevolent blue eyes, too small and misplaced.

She remembered how she had sat rigidly on the edge of the sofa as the dog wandered through the house, sniffing. She was deeply offended. This was the house in which she had been born, had raised a family, and in which she would die. She would have been offended if a stranger had even looked at the house with such selfish intensity. To have this odd animal insanely smelling the objects that were so much a part of her life was intolerable.

The dog had gone upstairs. He was probably in her bedroom. Tears came to her eyes. And then he was next to her on the sofa, his stiff-haired body pressing against her arm. She began to sob, and then felt his sharp-clawed paws pressing against her thin shoulder. His tongue was on her cheek.

She shuddered, remembering something that had happened more than fifty years before. She had been in a sunny grade-school classroom. Plump Miss Rosen was peering through thick-lensed glasses and saying, 'Never put money in your mouth. Money is covered with germs. And never let a dog lick you. A dog uses its tongue as toilet paper.'

It was the first time Mrs. Prescott had consciously recalled the teacher's words, but she realized that she had told her own children the same thing about money, and she had never allowed them to own a dog.

Her vision still dulled by tears, she put her hands on Baxter's body and tried to push him away. She could feel his rapid heartbeat, and her hand accidentally brushed against his genitals. She stopped struggling with him. She put her hands against her face and leaned limply against the back of the sofa. The dog settled in her lap. Gradually her tears subsided as she felt the animal's warmth spreading across her thighs. She lowered her hands. 'Baxter,' she whispered.

From that moment an accommodation existed. She could not refuse the dog's simple love, but she could not return it. She would tolerate it, as she had tolerated affection throughout her life: occasionally with appreciation, but never with trust.

And yet recently there had been evenings such as this one when she moved more eagerly than usual along the street; eager not so much to see the dog as to let him see her.

She was in her own block now. The thick foliage of old elms arched above her, forming a shadowy tunnel and obscuring the upper stories of the tall, ornate houses.

She had been born in one of these houses, when the trees were no taller than a man; when full sunlight could reach the asphalt of the road, softening it on summer afternoons. She remembered August days when she and her friends had walked barefoot on the asphalt, feeling it yield slightly against their weight. The other children would move quickly across the road, lifting their legs high as the heat stung the pale flesh of their feet. She was the only one who would stand motionless, defying the heat. It was then, perhaps, that she began to recognize the attraction discomfort held for her.

She understood Hawley Street in a way she had never understood her husband or children. These two rows of houses seemed to her to have an importance that their inhabitants never quite achieved. The night Mr. Raymond's house burned, she had stood in the cold darkness, weeping before the flames. Years later, when Mr. Raymond died, she stood dry-eyed at his graveside.

The block was a challenge that its people could not avoid. They would adapt to it as she had, or they would leave. Did the new young couple across the street realize that? Perhaps. They had chosen it over the suburbs and the city. But their principal interest was still themselves. They thought they could sustain that interest. They weren't aware of mortality or adversity. That awareness would come.

Mrs. Prescott smiled. I'm home, she thought. I'll fry a lamb chop, telephone my daughter, and perhaps watch television. And Baxter will follow me about in his fond, mindless way.

She would sleep contentedly, feeling the strength of the old house surrounding her, not expecting the morning to be in any way exceptional.

3

I am not comfortable in the night. I sometimes envy the old woman, who sleeps so complacently. The hurrying footsteps, the outcries, and the dozens of inexplicable sounds that disturb me do not affect her.

At first I found it hard to believe that a creature could be as insensitive as she is. She can detect only the most obvious sounds and odors. She spends a remarkable amount of time looking at things, and she murmurs pointlessly and almost continuously at me and at the people we meet.

Yet she can ignore the night. She is not disturbed by the thought of prowling cats, who move so confidently and silently through the darkness. She doesn't seem to realize that night creatures cannot be trusted, and sometimes I must cry out to warn her that strangers are dangerously close.

Perhaps she would sleep less soundly if she were not protected by this elaborate house. I find the house fascinating and comfortable, but it does not make me feel secure. It contains many traces of former inhabitants—people who will never return. Obviously it is the house that is safe and permanent; not those who live in it.

Each night, before the old lady is ready to sleep, she opens the back door and lets me go out into the night. My bladder contracts, my nostrils dilate, and I rush about the redolent, overgrown yard. In the darkness there are no visual distractions. I put my nose to the ground and concentrate fully on the scents that seem so rich in contrast to the staleness of the house.

I go first to the spot where I often find fresh rat droppings. I leave my own scent there, hardly taking time to raise my leg. There is so much territory to examine, and the old lady allows me so little time. There are nights, particularly when I have found traces of an unidentifiable creature, when she must force me back into the house, pulling at my collar and whining at me impatiently.

We go upstairs then. She locks herself in the bathroom and does the things that I am not allowed to witness. I lie on the bed and recall the experiences I have just had. There was a time when these recollections would stay with me all night. But now, after the old woman is in bed and her breathing has become noisy, I leave the bedroom. I go down to the living-room, my claws clicking on the shiny bare wood of the stairs. I go to the window and watch the house across the street until it is in darkness.

Then I lie on the sofa and think of the couple. I wait to hear the faint, peculiar sounds they make in the darkness. If I were living with them I think there would be no acts I would not be allowed to witness.

I go back up the stairs and sit at the side of the old woman's bed. I stare at her dim figure. I listen to her harsh breathing. And I wait for morning.

Two

One of the things Mrs. Prescott resented about Baxter was the way he interfered with her morning routine. After the death of her husband she had formed the habit of awakening slowly, letting consciousness come and go in irregular waves. Her first thoughts were no longer of someone else's needs, but of herself and the present moment.

She had never been a sensual person, and she had seldom been expected to behave like one. Yet she had begun to rediscover in the first moments of consciousness each morning the pleasures of simple sensation. It pleased her to notice the slightly cooler temperature of her body below the line where her nightgown ended. There were mornings when the nightgown had worked itself almost up to her waist, and she felt a sexual pleasure that, although mild, was more meaningful than any she had experienced with a man. I am, she would think, a person who appreciates subtleties.

Also, in these moments, she enjoyed opening her eyes partially and briefly—not enough to allow an image to register, but just enough to let herself feel the complex process of vision begin. The simple perception of formless light pleased her.

At such times she occasionally wondered whether she might be something other than the commonplace person she seemed to herself when fully awake.

Baxter's arrival ended such speculation. He was there

beside her bed each morning, whimpering and bringing her immediately into the reality of the world they shared. What exactly did they share? He was at her bedside now. When she opened her eyes his whimpering stopped, and his tail began to scrape back and forth across the floor.

He's pleased that I'm awake, she thought. But would he be any less pleased if I were some other person? She had sometimes wondered the same thing about her husband and her children. She was the one who fed them and consoled them, and they were grateful in varying degrees. Perhaps they had even loved her, but if so it was a destructive love— not the harmless kind of affection she sensed in Baxter.

Mrs. Prescott looked into the dog's strange eyes. It stared at her with a directness she had never seen in a human expression. She remembered how her husband had seldom looked directly into her eyes. He had looked at her face as if it had been her elbow. Her eyes could have been plaster; a detail of an uninteresting surface.

It was in this bedroom that he had first seen her without her clothes. He asked her to stand before him. He stared at her for perhaps five minutes, his gaze never moving above her shoulders until he noticed the tears falling on to her breasts.

Baxter could never insult me in that way, she thought. She drew back the covers and stood up. The dog ran excitedly to the doorway and stopped, waiting for her to follow him down the stairs. Instead of following him, she stood in the center of the floor and removed her nightgown. She watched Baxter carefully. He was staring into her eyes. She smiled and reached for her robe.

From the sidewalk came the tapping and scraping of Mr. Cuzzo's cane. Each morning he moved slowly and noisily along the street, displaying his pain to the neighborhood, mumbling about the past. Mrs. Prescott had never liked him, but she did respect the fact that he paid young men to paint and repair his house, to cut the lawn, and to plant flowers. It disturbed her that he could no longer walk to the end of the block, but that was because he was only two years older than she was.

Baxter whined. Mrs. Prescott tightened the belt of her robe and walked out of her bedroom. The dog usually ran down the stairs ahead of her, but this morning he did not seem to want to leave her. She paused at the head of the stairs, as she did each morning. It was the moment when she was reminded of the beauty of the old house. She had seldom in her life been offered the tributes that people pay to personal beauty. And she mistrusted those who made such gestures. The dog rubbed against her ankle. Perhaps I have been wrong, she thought.

And then Baxter circled behind her. Before she could turn to see why he was hesitating, she felt his weight against her calves. Her knees bent, and she pitched forward.

As she twisted, trying to regain her balance, she caught a glimpse of Baxter. She wondered whether his eyes were reflecting betrayal or stupidity. Her right hand brushed against the oak paneling she had polished so many times. And for a moment that seemed the longest of her life, she was suspended in the space of the old house. I have loved it, she thought. Her left hand reached for the rungs of the ornately carved banister, but they were beyond her grip. The ceiling moved slowly before her eyes, then the landing window, which was glowing in the morning light. How satisfying to see these things now, to be engulfed by them. And then the stairs. She had never wanted them carpeted. They were strong and handsome, and now the polished oak was just inches from her head. She closed her eyes and drew in her breath. There was a faint aroma of floor polish. She smiled. 'I was not wrong,' she whispered.

2

Mr. Cuzzo paused, leaning on his cane and squinting at the Prescott house. He had always considered a dog's bark the ugliest of all noises. What had come over Eileen Prescott? She had never been one to tolerate ugliness around her, and yet she was allowing that creature to stand on her sofa and make that unbearable noise. She was getting old.

He put both hands on the cane and rested the bulge of his stomach against it. He wanted to go on, but he was unable even to inch forward now. Without the cane he would not have been able to stand. He waited for his strength to return, and he thought of Eileen Prescott. An unattractive woman who disliked unattractiveness in others. A healthy woman who disliked those who were unhealthy. She had never allowed Mr. Cuzzo to like her. He never saw her without remembering that day in her garage. They had been wearing bathing suits. How old had he been? Ten? She had laughed at what he showed her. Did she ever remember that? Probably not. And perhaps it was wrong of him to remember such trivialities; wrong to watch, as he did, for the signs of her decline.

But there were mornings as he passed her house when he imagined alarming growths developing on her body; when he listened attentively for a cough. When they met on the street he questioned her carefully about the past, waiting for the day when she would hesitate and look confused.

He was encouraged when the dog began to live with her. It was perhaps the first crack in the wall of her independence. Now there was no doubt of it. The dog was beyond her control. How could she stand that yowling? And then it occurred to Mr. Cuzzo that the dog might be trying to get his attention. Maybe something was wrong. He pushed against his cane, moving his weight fully on to his legs, and turning to face the dog.

It barked without pause, clawing at the window. Obviously it was desperate, and obviously Mrs. Prescott would have stopped it if she had been able to. Mr. Cuzzo was helpless. His strength was not returning. He leaned once more against his cane and stared at the dog. So ugly. This was the creature she allowed to love her.

Mr. Cuzzo's eyes were moist.

3

I suppose they have become dominant merely because there are so many of them. There is no other explanation. They are so awkward and defenseless. The woman was old, I admit, but even if she had been younger she wouldn't have been agile enough to recover her balance. There can be no doubt it is a mistake to walk upright. If the old woman had walked on all fours, or at least had crouched, she would not be lying twisted and unbreathing on the landing now.

It was a minute or two before her breathing stopped. She murmured something in those last moments—not the noises one makes when in pain, but the monotonous gabble that she and her kind make almost continuously. I don't think I'll ever understand why they are so devoted to making those sounds. It may be that they comfort and reassure themselves that way. They are very insecure.

I believe the couple are still in their house. I want them to be the ones to discover what has happened. I want them to take me to their house. The old fat man has heard me, but he won't come to see what has happened. He is a useless creature. If he had to find his own food he could not survive more than a few days. The steps to the front porch are as forbidding to him as if they were a wall of flame. Yet someone tolerates him; is loyal to him. People have a great capacity for loyalty to those who seem to depend on them. I have benefitted from that loyalty, but I don't understand it. Urinate on their carpets, chew up one of the objects they endlessly accumulate. They sometimes punish, but in their loyalty they always forgive. Does their loyalty have any limits? Some day I'll know. Soon, perhaps.

Three

John and Nancy Grafton lay half awake, listening to the sound of muffled barking. The windows behind them were bright with leaf-filtered sunlight. The covers were thrown back, and their bodies were faintly striped with shadows cast by the vertical bars at the head of the massive brass bed. John disliked the bed. It stood high off the floor, isolating and confining. It was designed by someone with strange attitudes, he thought. A device for punishment, or at least for pleasures that didn't match his. Bars to which wrists and ankles could be tied.

His wife liked the bed, as she liked the elaborate relic of a house that contained it. Her world was more palpable than his. It pleased her to notice the worn edges of the stairs, to imagine the people who had walked there before her.

Her world was also moral. It was not necessarily a virtuous world, but it was one that allowed the possibility of individual virtue. John had always behaved well by most standards, but the standards were never his own. Last year, in graduate school, he came to realize that he was the kind of person who would never have his own standards; he would do what others expected of him: his parents, his teachers, his friends, policemen, sales clerks, almost anyone. Even pets.

He had decided his only chance for happiness was to concentrate on pleasing only one person: the best person he knew. That person was Nancy, who had brought them to

26

this town and had introduced him to the kind of happiness that resulted from limited choices. Only occasionally did he recall that many people who were honored and remembered had not been happy people.

His pleasure was intense this morning. He was pleased merely to have Nancy lying beside him. She was awake now, he knew, although she had not moved or spoken. He sensed the slight tension that consciousness had brought to her body, and he sensed her sexual arousal. She would speak soon. Words were part of the sex act for her: a prologue and epilogue. Aural sex. Her words would be commonplace or frivolous, but her intention would be serious.

'You don't like dogs, do you?' she asked.

'Sensible people don't.'

John opened his eyes and turned his head slightly to look at her unfamiliarly thick body. She was four months pregnant. Her hand lay on the receding curve of her belly, her fingertips moving slowly across her sparse, reddish pubic hair. He replaced her hand with his own.

Nancy shivered. The dog was howling now. It was the old woman's dog. She remembered meeting them on the street. They had seemed so strange together: the old woman careful, resentful; the dog affectionate, uninhibited. Its cold nose against her foot. Moist.

'What's wrong with dogs?'

'They're parasites. They inspire third-rate emotions.'

He likes dogs, Nancy thought. This is a game. He's inventing pleasures. 'What else?' she asked.

'They defecate in public.'

'Yes.'

'And copulate.'

'Yes, my darling.'

Her eyes were closed. The bed creaked slightly as her husband's weight shifted. Then his cheek was on her thigh. Abrasive, bristly.

He mumbled, 'They sniff. They lick.'

'Yes, my darling.'

Soon she rolled over on to her stomach. Her hands grasped the bars at the head of the bed. And then she was kneeling.

'You wouldn't want a dog?' she asked.

'It would watch us.'

'Yes, my dearest, it would watch.' She lowered her head, her hair spilling across the pillow. 'What would it think?'

'The unspeakable.' He was behind her, his hands on her hips.

'Yes. Oh, yes.'

'Bitch. My bitch.'

2

On the street below, in the shadow of the elms, Mr. Cuzzo leaned on his cane and stared at Mrs. Prescott's window. The dog's pale, baying head was dimly visible behind the curtains. To the old man, through his tears, the animal looked ghostly and more sinister than anything he had ever seen.

3

'Young man?'

Mr. Cuzzo watched gratefully as John Grafton stepped out of his front door.

'Young man, I need your help.' How easily he moves, the old man thought. How long did it take him to get ready to leave the house? No surgical appliances to put in place. No salves to apply; no capsules to swallow; no special diet to prepare. Coffee. A few clothes.

'What can I do for you?' John asked. He respected the old

man, for he realized his mere appearance on the street was an act of courage. But he preferred not to look at him.

'There's something wrong in Mrs. Prescott's house.'

'Are you sure?'

'I'm sure. It's the dog. She'd stop it if she could.'

John thought Mr. Cuzzo was probably mistaken; just searching for drama. 'You'd better rest,' he said, and helped him to the porch. He lowered him to the steps, grasping an arm that felt like a rubber tube not quite full of water. 'Shall I call the police?'

'No. Go in.'

'Is that legal?'

'It's necessary.'

The barking was louder, harsher.

John went up the steps and tried the front door. It was locked. He walked across the porch to the window, brushing against an old glider that was suspended from rusty chains. The glider moved gently from side to side. Mr. Cuzzo watched it, remembering an evening when he had sat there with Mrs. Prescott (Miss Haley then). He had not known what to say to her, and he was afraid to touch her. They had rocked slowly amid the sounds of crickets and the neighbors' radios.

John pushed on the window-frame. It moved slowly upward. Baxter stopped barking and began to lick the man's hands.

The house was silent.

John called out, 'Mrs. Prescott?'

Across the street his wife stood on their porch, looking uneasily at him.

John moved awkwardly through the window and over the sofa. The dog ran to the foot of the stairs and sat looking back at him.

John stood in the center of the room. It's like a church, he thought: substantial, under-used; a place for ceremonies.

It was much like the house his wife had chosen for them.

It was a choice he objected to at first, sensing something idle and romantic in it; a feature article in a Sunday supplement. But he knew his sense of place had always been feeble. He had lived in city apartments, college dormitories, country cabins, and the only difference he noticed was in degrees of comfort. He believed it was a weakness to have one's moods and thoughts affected significantly by one's surroundings.

He started towards the waiting dog, but paused before the marble-mantled fireplace, which was crowded with photographs. He felt a sense of guilt and discomfort in staring at these preserved private moments. The pictures were not the decorative work of professional photographers; they were harshly lighted images of people staring at other people. Mrs. Prescott was in most of the snapshots, plain, distrustful, her hands never relaxed.

Baxter barked.

John went to stand next to the dog at the foot of the stairs. On the landing, extending over the top stair, was Mrs. Prescott's hand, relaxed and graceful as it had never been in life. John walked slowly up the stairs and took Mrs. Prescott's wrist in his fingers. He avoided looking directly at her body, but he was aware of a grotesquely twisted leg protruding from a worn robe. After a minute he went down to the telephone and asked the operator for the number of the nearest hospital.

Baxter stood next to him for a moment, his tail thrashing wildly. And then the dog ran across the room, leaped through the open window, rushed past Mr. Cuzzo, and crossed the street to where John's wife stood.

On his way to unlock the front door, John paused again before the photographs. The most recent of them seemed to be the one that showed Mrs. Prescott standing at the entrance of the house, on the top of the porch stairs. Baxter was next to her, standing on his hind legs, his strong front legs pushing against her thigh.

4

Florence Rapp, Mrs. Prescott's daughter, was slumped heavily on the sofa in her mother's parlor. Her legs were as neatly crossed as her bulky thighs would permit. She sipped from a large glass of whiskey and ice. She spoke with a lack of animation that seemed habitual; not the result of grief or strain. 'Would you like to keep the dog? It seems fond of you.'

John Grafton looked questioningly at his wife. She wants the dog, he thought. She needs affection less complicated than mine; less demanding than the child's will be.

'You're sure you don't want it for yourself, Mrs. Rapp?' Nancy asked.

'No.' Her answer was emphatic. She paused, as if deciding whether to explain her reasons. Finally, she merely said, 'I don't care for them.' She might have been speaking of cockroaches.

'I thought your mother told us you bred them,' John said.

'My husband does. It's one of our differences.'

Probably one of many, Nancy thought, and then asked, 'Is the breed good with children?'

'Supposedly. They were bred as fighters originally, but they seem docile enough these days. Baxter has a flaw, but I don't think it's psychological.'

'What is it?' John asked.

'His blue eyes. He's an excellent specimen of bull terrierdom in almost every other respect, but the blue eyes would disqualify him in a show. It's what's called a genetic shadow—a trait that just appears from somewhere out of the past. So, what my husband hoped would be Champion Baxter's Angel ... by Lord Baxter out of Bright Angel ... becomes merely Baxter and is condemned to pethood. In any case, I hope you'll take him. I feel I owe you something.

Mother might have been there for days if you hadn't found her.'

'Baxter should get the credit,' John said.

'Maybe we should have called him Lassie,' Mrs. Rapp said into her nearly empty glass.

John smiled. 'Well, Laddie, at least.'

Nancy was not smiling. 'We'd very much like to have him.'

'Done,' said Mrs. Rapp. She slid an ice cube into her mouth and crunched it between gold-filled molars. Take the beast, she thought. Take the people, the houses, the trees. Have as many pregnancies and ideals as you can manage; you won't save any of it. Something or someone will defeat you.

John stood up. There was no point in watching Mrs. Rapp get any drunker. 'We should be going, I think.' He didn't see any reason either to offer sympathies, at least not for the death of her mother. Perhaps for some other, earlier loss. But he didn't know what that might have been.

Nancy was next to him. 'Let us know if there is anything we can do. We'll keep an eye on the house.'

Mrs. Rapp's heavy legs uncrossed involuntarily, and her head jerked back slightly. 'We'll sell it,' she said.

'And thank you for the dog,' John said. 'I think it will be happy with us.'

Mrs. Rapp said seriously, 'It needs discipline.'

We all do, John thought.

The couple went to the door. The dog lay in the center of the room, looking from Mrs. Rapp to the couple. He was trembling.

'Baxter,' Nancy said. 'Come along, Baxter. You have a new home.'

In the moment before the dog sprang towards the door he deposited on the intricately patterned old rug a small rivulet of urine. Only Mrs. Rapp noticed. After Baxter and the couple were gone she sat staring at the floor and watching the stain darken and spread.

Four

My pleasure increases endlessly. The woman has stopped going off with the man during the day, and she is with me almost constantly. She is attentive, and really quite intelligent. She has learned to feed me fresh, raw meat. She brings me large, mysterious bones, which I crack fiercely, feeling pride and pleasure in the strength of my teeth and jaws. She delights in touching me, and she has no secrets from me. We often lie on her bed in the warm afternoon, dozing and listening to the birds and insects.

The man is less interested in me, but he respects my skills. Sometimes at dusk, in the overgrown back yard, I capture a rat. I shake it, listening to its terrified squeals before I tighten my jaws and feel it go limp. I carry it to the back porch and lay it carefully before the door. The man sometimes praises me for my prowess, but I can sense his uneasiness. I continue the practice, however, sometimes presenting them with two or three little corpses, laid out neatly side by side. It helps the couple understand me.

I sometimes remember the old lady, but I never regret having interfered with her. I think of her fondly. She taught me that one should constantly try to improve one's position in life. I think there are many of my kind who have never learned that lesson. I see them when the woman and I take our walks. I sense their boredom, and when they enviously try to sniff me I draw back my lips and show them my strong teeth. The most pitiable are those that wander alone, without the charm to have attracted even an old, dull-eyed person; without the cleverness to have chosen a devoted young couple, as I have. They live only for the moment.

Almost at will now I can think beyond the moment, and I understand that conditions change; that I must be able to control those changes. The young woman, for example, is changing. Her body is becoming thicker and thicker, and there is an added scent about her that I find unpleasant. It is almost as if she had the scent of two people.

I don't understand it. But I no longer fear things that I don't understand.

2

It was Saturday morning. John and Nancy were drinking coffee in the large, dark parlor. A breeze moved through the screened windows, bringing the aroma of freshly cut grass. The sound of a lawn-mower came from next door. Mr. Best, their large, dour black neighbour, had begun his weekend landscaping devotions.

Mr. Best resented the Graftons, and he despised their weed-clogged back yard. Sometimes during the week, sitting bored at his desk in his insurance office, he would think of the weed seeds drifting from the Graftons' little meadow on to his velvety grass and meticulously planned flower borders.

Every person must have some pride, he thought. He had no idea what the Graftons took pride in. Certainly not in their own appearance or in the appearance of their possessions. Maybe they were proud of their thoughts or their feelings; or maybe just of their youth. He had never spoken to them.

'We should do something about the back yard, John.'

'Do what?'

'Make it less . . . luxuriant. And get rid of some of the wildlife.'

'Baxter wouldn't approve.'

'Baxter's a dog.'

Nancy sat in the tattered Morris chair, resenting her discomfort. There was a time when she had thought of herself as a person who could be indifferent to discomfort, but now, late in her pregnancy, she knew she could only tolerate distress, not ignore it.

Baxter was deep in the process of digesting his breakfast. He lay with his lower jaw flat against the floor. He had opened his eyes briefly at the sound of his name.

'I'll build a pond in the yard,' John said.

'Sure, John.'

'With a waterfall. You don't have to mow a pond.'

'You have to build it.'

'We could have some water lilies. Monet.'

John had majored in art history, but he had been more interested in books than in paintings or sculpture. Names, dates and titles impressed him. He wrote long, accurately researched papers that were overwhelmingly lacking in significance. Whenever he visited a museum his hands swelled to the point of immobility. He had been told he could become a superior teacher.

He looked at Nancy. Pregnancy had affected her appearance in unexpected ways. Her fingers seemed shorter, although not thicker. Her face seemed thinner than before. There were distortions, but not of essential features. Exaggerations. A caricature. Who were the important caricaturists? He thought that the word itself was derived from an artist's name: an Italian. That's all he could remember about the subject. That part of him was gone. Instead there was an unruly yard to consider. It's an improvement, he thought.

'I'll start it today,' he said.

'Start what?' Nancy's eyes had been closed.

'The pond.'

'Yes. That's a good idea, darling.'

She was wrong.

3

From the moment John turned over the first clump of earth in the yard, he felt both an urgency and a distaste about the project. The soil was rich with decayed vegetation, fetid and wormy. Baxter joined in the digging, clawing frantically, scattering earth behind him, and pausing occasionally to sniff and examine an object he uncovered.

The pond became a matter of significance in the neighborhood. Faces appeared and lingered in windows that overlooked the Grafton yard. Mr. Cuzzo learned to pause in his daily walks at a point between houses, where he could see the excavation. People meeting on the street spoke no longer of Mrs. Prescott's death, but of the young man who worked shirtless and sweating each evening until sunset.

Mr. Best would often be working in the yard next door; delicately pruning, smoothing, raking. John was afraid of black men. His fear was not the result of a complex prejudice. He supposed Mr. Best differed significantly from most white men only in the darkness of his skin. It was the darkness that John feared. He was intimidated in the same way he would have been by a black-skinned apple.

The two men began to speak, cautiously and infrequently, facing each other over their shared fence.

John would pause in his work to look at other back yards. They're like the backs of minds, he thought. They reveal differing degrees of use and order: in one an old lady's five-and-ten underclothes were drying on a slack line: knee-length pink drawers; knitted vests. In another a venerable pear-tree supported a small crop of inedible fruit. In Mr. Best's there was brightness and symmetry.

Nancy watched the project from the back porch, her swollen body eased into an old cane-backed rocker. She was disturbed. At first she thought she merely resented losing so much of her husband's time and attention.

But then one night she realized that the pond itself offended her. She had been unable to sleep, and had gone to the kitchen to warm some milk. Baxter followed her. While the milk heated she stood looking out of the window. The sharp-rocked waterfall and pool basin were nearly in their final form. In the bright moonlight the structure looked forbidding: a site for unpleasantness.

She saw a vague, pale form. It lingered at the edge of the pool's basin briefly and then vanished. She assumed it had been Baxter. But then, startled, she felt the dog push against her leg, and she realized she had not let it out.

The milk had scalded.

The next day she dragged the rocking-chair from the back porch into the parlor. And from then until the pool was finished she spent her evenings sitting inside while her husband worked in the yard.

Baxter sat with her, going occasionally into the kitchen to sit before the screen door to watch her husband work. The dog, which seemed to have lost its original curiosity over the construction of the pool, was restless and nervous.

We're all nervous, Nancy thought. It's the baby. John claimed he was working on the pond so intently because he wanted it finished before the cold weather set in. But Nancy knew it was simple evasion. Her presence unsettled him. He could not accept this gross body, which was neither the woman he had loved nor the child he would love. He needed distraction until one became two.

Five

I am the bond between the man and the woman. Unlike me, they are unstable creatures. I go from one to the other, reassuring them, accepting the affection they no longer give easily to each other. And although my pleasure in being with them is less simple than it was originally, I don't regret my choice. It is as if they had been waiting for a third party to complete their lives.

There are acts they no longer perform. They lie in the dark, the man smelling of fatigue, the woman of the illness that has changed her body. They do not touch and join. They sometimes murmur briefly, and they soon sleep.

The man realizes, as I do, that the earth has a mystery and power that cannot be found in houses. He has taught me about time. Together in the yard we uncover traces of those who lived before the houses existed. An odor of decay more pungent and complex than the odors of life; small bones; fragments of abandoned possessions; a concentration of the aroma that arose from the old woman as she lay on the landing of the stairs: the odor of death. It is an odor that pleases me.

The man has done a strange thing, though. He has covered the earth with stones and water. I don't know why he should do such a thing. He has destroyed the growing things and has left me very little room to run in.

He doesn't seem to fear water as I do. Each morning, in the room of the house that interests me least, he sprays himself with water, removing his distinctive, attractive scent and applying one that repels me. The woman is even more reckless than the man. Despite her illness, which has made her so awkward, she immerses her heavy body completely in water. It is one of her more foolish habits.

The woman's illness is strange. She must be uncomfortable, yet she smiles and seems pleased in a self-concerned way. There is a new gentleness in her touch.

It comforts me to know that the man and woman do not possess the cleverness or strength I once imagined they had. They rely on me in many ways, and their affection for me is stronger than ever. I wouldn't want anything to interfere with that.

2

Mr. Cuzzo paused and pushed aside a brown, fallen elm-leaf with his cane. It was a lavish use of energy for him, but he was celebrating the change of season. He had walked half a block without any involuntary pauses. He had stopped now only to look between the Grafton and Best houses at the pond. It was completed now, he supposed. Water spilled and collected, reflecting the sunlight. Something new on the block; something novel. And soon a child would be born. Mr. Cuzzo was not sure he approved. A neighborhood should produce only one generation; one set of structures; one set of passions and tragedies. There is no tragedy for us, he thought; just misfortune. Tragedy is for the young. We should not have to witness it.

He stood motionless, staring. Images registered dully: the gold of chrysanthemums in Mr. Best's yard; the rust of leaves floating on the Graftons' pond. And then Baxter appeared, his white form and quick movement confusing the old man momentarily. The dog stared across the street and began to bark.

Mr. Cuzzo turned away and continued haltingly down the street. 'We should not have to witness it,' he mumbled.

3

Long before he completed the pond, John found himself thinking what he had thought too often in his life: Why am I doing this? He wanted to be in the parlor with Nancy, but he felt it was more important to show her he was capable of facing the disagreeable. It was an ordeal that he endured; an ordeal to match her own.

And then it was finished. There was no announcement; he merely joined her in the parlor one night at the time he usually went out into the yard. Nancy was lying on the sofa, the profile of her body like a strange landscape. John sat on the floor and took her hand; kissed it.

'I want it to be born in this house,' she said.

'Is that allowed?'

'I've made arrangements.'

She had been seeing a doctor who had his offices near by in one of the neighborhood houses. John disapproved of him: weak-eyed, semi-retired, too comfortable with death. The midhusband, he called him.

'Is it safe, Nancy?'

'It's right.'

She didn't want her child to open its eyes to fluorescent light. 'I'm healthy,' she said.

She drew up the skirt of her loose dress and put her husband's hand on her distended body. She felt his resistance, his reluctance to touch the shiny, taut flesh.

He looked away from her, trying to understand his fear. His eyes met the mysterious blue eyes of Baxter, who lay confidently at Nancy's feet.

In the deepening shadows of the yard, water trickled over rocks into the dark pool.

Six

I have been betrayed. I lie in the dark garage, a filthy rug beneath me, freezing drafts blowing across my body. I no longer have a sense of the present. I constantly relive that disastrous day.

It began with the woman's gasps. She lay on the bed, her face distorted, her hands clutching at the bedspread. I tried to comfort her, to lick her hand. But the man forced me from the room. It was the first time he had touched me in anger. I stood outside the closed door, listening to the woman's cries and the man's muted muttering.

And then the strangers arrived: a feeble man and a young woman wearing white shoes. They both smelled of pungent, lifeless substances. I challenged them, and once more my man touched me in anger. He forced me out into the back yard. I was frantic. I wanted to be with the woman. I resented the presence of the strangers. I began to call out to them. Soon the man was back, but instead of letting me in he leaned over and struck me. I felt the muscles of my chest tighten. My jaws opened. If he hadn't withdrawn his hand I think I would have bitten him. He was making harsh, threatening noises. It occurred to me for the first time since the death of the old woman how vulnerable people are to attack. They are not to be feared. But in their moments of instability they are to be pitied. I made myself remember his previous devotion, and I overcame my anger.

I moved restlessly about the yard, stopping occasionally

to listen for sounds from the house. There were barely audible mumblings interspersed with the woman's sharp gasps and moans. And then I heard the new voice. Its sound was piercing and shapeless; a declaration of helplessness. It was a voice I came to despise.

Several days passed before I was allowed to see the child. They were days of neglect. The woman in the white shoes fed me and kept me from the bedroom. I could smell her fear of me. The child's squealing became the dominant sound in the house, waking us in the middle of the night, never letting us forget its presence.

Then one day the man carried me into the bedroom. The woman, slender again and smiling, stood beside us. There, in a small, cage-like bed was the tiny creature; toothless and almost hairless. I had never seen anything that looked more weak or less intelligent. I looked at the man and woman. They had an appearance of pride rather than shame, and I realized that my life with them would be unbearable as long as the child was with us.

And so I lie in the garage and endlessly consider my new situation. Snow is deep in the yard, concealing the odors of life. The chilling wind that sweeps over me is not as disturbing as the mewling of the child.

There are two courses open to me. I can leave the couple or I can rid them of the child. The risks of leaving are great. I do not want a new, unpredictable life. I want to restore our old happiness. But they guard the child carefully. That might not always be so, however. I think if I am amiable and patient an opportunity will come.

2

Nancy Grafton unbuttoned her blouse and bared her left breast. Her son, Charles, took the nipple eagerly into his small, wet mouth. Both mother and child closed their eyes in contentment.

John watched them intently. He remembered the first time Nancy had unbuttoned her blouse for him. They had been sitting across the dinner table in her apartment, talking and sipping cognac. She had moved deliberately and seriously, exposing her breasts for just a moment, not as provocation, but as a sign. He had never fully understood the gesture, and the sight of her breasts had always brought him a complex pleasure that was more interesting than simple eroticism.

But now, seeing her with the child, he realized that that particular pleasure was gone and would not return.

'Poor Baxter,' Nancy said, her eyes still closed.

'He'll be okay. I think he's starting to get used to things.'

'I hadn't realized he was so sensitive.'

'He likes you, that's all,' John said. 'I'm a little jealous myself, and I had a few months to get used to the idea.'

'You're not going to start sleeping in the garage, though?'

'Not unless you are.'

Despite her husband's assurances about the dog, Nancy was frightened by the strength of Baxter's jealousy. There's no subtlety in the animal's emotions, she thought. And without the tempering of subtleties, the dog's emotions could be stronger than hers or John's. She hoped the emotion the dog felt was love for her and not hatred for the child.

Nancy looked at Baxter. He was lying in a corner of the room, pale in the shadows, his deep-set eyes staring at either her or the baby.

'Baxter,' she said.

His ears moved and his tail wagged hesitantly, yet he made no move to come to her. But that night he slept in the house for the first time since the birth of the child.

The next morning the dog was waiting for Nancy outside the bedroom. Smiling, she knelt next to him and stroked his muscular body. 'You've made your decision, haven't you?' she said.

3

Winter altered the neighborhood. Life became more secretive; dormancy and patience flourished. The flaws in houses and bodies became more apparent in the harsh light that was reflected from snow rather than filtered by leaves.

Mr. Cuzzo abandoned his walks. He sat at his window, tapping the glass with his cane when an acquaintance passed.

Mr. Best, with ruler and carefully sharpened pencil, drew diagrams of his garden area; looked again and again at the garish pages of seed catalogs.

The infant Charles Grafton slept, sucked, cried, and gradually began to distinguish the things that surrounded him. Among those things was the white creature, which was so different from the man and woman, and which watched him so attentively.

Seven

The child is not normal. I think that explains why the man and woman lavish such attention on it. They do not love it, they pity it; they feel guilt for having produced it. The snow has gone, the earth is once more soft and fragrant, and still the child is helpless. Surely such a condition cannot be normal, even among men and women.

My life has been difficult, but there have been rewards. I have learned, for example, that I can be patient; not as patient as the man and woman, but their kind of patience is no virtue.

I believe the moment I have waited for is near. The woman has begun to leave the child alone with me. I think she even imagines I will help her to protect it. There are more and more opportunities for me to do what must be done.

What I have to consider carefully is the method. The choice of means seemed unlimited at first. The child has no cunning and no strength. In its mindlessness it would soon destroy itself if it were not watched and tended constantly. But then I realized the event should meet two requirements: it should be unobserved, and it should appear to be the result of one of the child's many stupidities.

The answer came to me this morning, I believe. I was lying in the warm grass of the back yard, listening to sounds that have been absent: the whine of insects, the pleasing, high-pitched song of certain birds. I was thinking about the strangeness of birds. Even though they have always been respectful of me, there is something about them that makes me uneasy. I wondered whether I would kill one if I had the opportunity.

I heard the woman coming into the yard, and I opened my eyes. She spread a blanket on the grass, and then she brought the child out and sat down on the blanket with it. The child flailed its arms and legs in its aimless way, making the gurgling sounds that seem to indicate pleasure. It has teeth now; only a few and hardly worthy of the name, but I was relieved when they appeared.

Within the house, the telephone rang. The woman stood up. She leaned over to pick up the child, hesitated, then straightened up and went into the house. I watched the child. In the background the sun sparkled on the water of the pool. The baby was lying on its stomach. Then it did something I had never seen it do before: it raised itself on to its hands and knees and moved forward. It collapsed after a moment, but it was enough to show me a moment in the future: the moment when the child would be found in the pool. I would be at the edge of the water, having summoned help too late.

2

'He's begun to crawl,' Nancy said.

'That's good,' John said. He meant it. In recent weeks he had begun to wonder whether his son might be abnormally slow in developing. The growth that seemed so obvious in the beginning was hardly noticeable now. He sometimes remembered the phrase Mrs. Rapp had used about Baxter: a genetic shadow. Had there been something unnatural lurking within himself or his wife? Something that had been passed on unseen for generations, infinitely patient, inexorable, that would now be given form? Something to be regretted or even dreaded?

'We'll need a playpen for him soon,' Nancy said.

'One of those cages?'

'Something like that.'

A little animal, John thought. Caged from the start. 'We've got plenty of spare rooms,' he said. 'Why don't I fix one up? Fill it with soft things. We could at least give him a cell, instead of a cage.'

'You could. But I want him to get outside, too. I don't think he's ready for swimming yet.'

John was silent. Nancy knew he didn't like to be reminded of the pool. It was evidence of the fear her pregnancy had produced in him. They both had been brought up to believe that such evidence had to be lived with, and so they lived with the pool, ignoring the uneasiness it brought them.

3

Mr. Best approved of the pool. To him it was evidence of industry and humanity. He believed people should grow things or make things. The selling of insurance had few satisfactions for him. He envied the people who had made the older houses in the town; who had shaped the banisters and fitted the parquet floors.

It was a Saturday morning, and his pleasure was intense. Meticulously he placed new plants into the dark earth, dampness seeping through the knees of his trousers, his nostrils tingling to the scent of nearby lilac blossoms.

Through the fence he saw the stocky white body of the dog; beyond that the child lay on a blue blanket. Bees hummed, and the water splashed over rocks. He heard the laughter of the couple, who had gone inside a few minutes earlier. They were upstairs.

Breeding, thought Mr. Best. He had no children; he wanted none. He had cross-bred plants and had seen the effects: occasionally admirable, but more often ridiculous or self-destructive. Now he left such matters to others. He would never have a rose named for him, but neither would he produce a monster.

As he got to his feet and started for his garage to mix some fertilizer, he noticed the dog get up and move towards the baby.

4

There had been a moment when it occurred to Nancy that they should not leave the child unprotected. But only a moment. She and John had been sitting on the blanket with the baby. Nancy was leaning back slightly, supporting herself on her hands, her left leg flat on the ground, and her right knee raised. John was facing her. As they sat, speaking sporadically, she noticed him glancing at her legs. Then she realized that her skirt had fallen back, and it was not only her legs he was looking at. During her pregnancy she had gotten out of the habit of wearing underwear.

Since the birth of the baby, John's lovemaking had been infrequent and calculated: only at night, only in bed, and with a leisurely quality that made it seem an act of duty rather than one of desire. And now, in the morning light, with the sounds of life about them, John's examination of her body was an exotic, instantly arousing act for Nancy.

When John stood up he was visibly aroused. He lifted her to her feet and held her body to his. Then there was the moment of concern for her son. 'We must be quick,' she said.

Minutes later, when the child cried out briefly, neither she nor John heard it. They heard only the short, nasty words they were repeating to each other as they approached the most self-absorbing of experiences.

When awareness of the world returned to them the sound they heard was an inhuman baying they had heard once before.

'Oh, my God,' John said, and looked at Nancy. They felt the beginnings of a guilt that would never leave them; a guilt that would later be reinforced by a suspicion too dreadful for either of them ever to mention.

5

I have misjudged the man and woman; there's no doubt of it now. They avoid me, and the smell of fear is always about them.

At first I thought they knew the truth, but that is impossible. I am certain they did not see me. I know what they were doing, and I know they see or hear nothing at those times.

The child was even weaker than I thought, and I acted quickly. I was careful not to touch its delicate skin with my teeth. It was a simple matter to grasp its clothing and drag it to the water. It cried out only briefly before I forced it under. It quickly went limp, and I stood back and watched until I knew its feeble hold on life was broken.

I knew that the man and woman would be distressed for a time, but I expected that after a few days they would begin to stroke me and would look at me with a new interest and respect. But I know now that that will never happen.

They are like the old woman. They no longer live in the present. They are obsessed with the past; not with past pleasures, but with past unpleasantness. Their love has been replaced by fear. It is possible that all humans are that way, but I cannot believe it. There must be some who see the world as I do; who know neither love nor fear. I think I can find such a person.

I sometimes wonder why I am not content to live a solitary life. It is not a matter of comfort, for it would not distress me to sleep in alleys and eat rats. There is another reason; one that I don't quite understand. It is as if there were a bond I must establish; a knowledge that I must share or give.

PART TWO

PART TWO

One

Carl Fine walked quickly along the quiet streets. It was dusk. In the houses he passed he could see families seated at dining-room tables, as he had been seated with his parents five minutes earlier. Carl was not interested in food, and he was not interested in his parents. Dinner, like so many other things in his life, was something he tolerated in silence and discomfort.

He noticed the change in light as he turned off Hawley Street. There were fewer trees now; smaller houses. Soon he was passing vacant lots, the city limits, and a scattering of factory buildings, most of them abandoned. And then he was entering the junk-yard. He felt comfortable for the first time that day.

He had discovered the junk-yard the previous summer, when he was twelve. He had sensed its importance immediately. Actually it was not a junk-yard. No one owned it, and nothing was bought or sold there. And it wasn't an official dumping ground. It was one of the inexplicable products of a civilized community: an unofficial, uncommercial place to discard things and to discover things.

To Carl it was the heart of the town; a place where the secrets of others were revealed and where his own could be kept. On the weekends and during the day other people came to the junk-yard to deposit something or to search. But in the evenings Carl was alone there except for an occasional stray dog or cat that moved quietly in the shadows.

Tonight, as always, there was the early touch of anxiety mingled with his pleasure. Had anyone discovered his secret? He made his way awkwardly among the mounds of metal, glass, wood and plastics. Occasionally he would step on something yielding and organic. He wouldn't stop to look down.

He could see his goal now. It seemed to be undisturbed: an apparently random heap of materials arranged around the shells of two smashed automobiles. He pushed aside a sheet of galvanized metal, revealing a large, dark chamber. He crawled inside the chamber, lit a candle and pulled the metal sheet back over the opening.

Stretching out on the musty rugs that lined the bottom of the chamber, Carl uncovered a metal box and searched through it in the flickering candlelight. He took from the box a bundle of photographs that had been clipped from magazines and books. He studied the clippings carefully, one after another. The same two people appeared in each of the photographs: a vapidly attractive blonde woman and a dark-haired, strange-eyed man. Eva Braun and Adolf Hitler.

Carl chose one of the photographs: Eva wearing a bathing suit and seated on a low stone wall, the Austrian Alps in the background. He rolled over on to his back and held the picture before him in his left hand. With his right hand he unbuckled his belt.

'Don't worry, Eva,' he said. 'We'll be safe here in the bunker.'

2

'Maybe we should get him a dog.'

'A dog?'

'You're worried because he doesn't have any friends. We can get him man's best.'

Jason and Sara Fine were seated at the dinner table, drinking coffee, smoking cigarettes, and talking about their son, Carl, who had just excused himself and hurried out of the house, leaving his dinner half eaten as he did almost every night.

Except for the hours she spent with her music, this was Sara's favorite time of day; the time when she most nearly shared her husband's patient, good-humored acceptance of existence. Sara had never quite enjoyed, or seen the point of, being alive. She preferred books and music to life. She was puzzled by most of the things people did, even in this little town. The futile energy; the persistence. The obese old man with the cane she saw on Hawley Street occasionally. Struggling. Why?

Jason liked to tell her about the people of the town. It was not gossip, exactly, because no matter how bizarre or ignoble the behavior he described, he would smile understandingly. Sara would try to smile with him, but she was never quite able to understand. Still, she enjoyed talking to her husband; enjoyed it more than anything else they did together.

But now there was Carl. Last year the boy had not been any trouble. They had bought him a camera and had equipped a darkroom for him in the basement. He spent hours there, producing remarkably few and decidedly odd prints. But the process gave him a discipline that he seemed to lack now.

'It's more than his not having friends,' Sara said. 'He's so unpredictable: charming sometimes, withdrawn at others. Lately he thinks he's a Nazi.'

Jason smiled. 'He *is* a Nazi,' he said. 'All thirteen-year-old boys are Nazis.'

'Were you one?'

'Of course. I saw the same war movies he's seeing on television now.' Jason's eyes narrowed, and the right side of his face began to twitch. 'Zo you von't talk, eh, Fräulein? Vee shall zee. Vee haff our vays.'

Sara was not amused.

Jason was not amused either. He suspected she was right about the boy. Carl had formed no bonds; not with them, not with anyone. It was not a tragedy, though. People live without bonds; or they find them late, in unexpected places. 'The point is,' he said, 'that Carl is a lot of things. He's a bright kid, he gets good grades and stays out of trouble. He gets along with people. His only problem is that he's an adolescent.'

'Were you serious about getting him a dog?'

'I'm not sure. I know where we can get one. John Grafton—the one whose little boy drowned—wants to get rid of his. It reminds his wife of the accident, he says.'

'What kind of dog?'

'I don't remember the breed. It's the kind General Patton had. White and strange-looking.'

Sara reached out to Carl's plate and pushed her cigarette into a mound of cold mashed potatoes. Her parents had been fond of dogs, and she had spent her childhood being followed about by a series of nudging, shedding, panting mongrels. What she had gained in companionship, she thought, had been canceled out by what she had lost in privacy. She was indifferent to dogs. 'We could ask Carl what he thinks,' she said.

'Would you mind having a dog around?' Jason asked.

'No. What harm could it do?'

3

As Carl left the junk-yard, stumbling through the darkness, a piece of metal embedded itself in the heel of his left shoe. He didn't try to remove it, enjoying both the limping unevenness it gave his gait and the sharp click it made as he hurried along the quiet streets.

Baxter, lying sleepless in the Graftons' garage, heard the clicking noise approach and recede along Hawley Street. It was an unfamiliar sound, and he growled as it passed.

4

Carl looked at his mother fiercely. 'Cheneral Patton?' he said. 'Zat *schwein*?'

'You don't have to do a routine. Just tell me whether you'd like to have a dog like that.'

Carl had seen the movie *Patton* four times. He remembered the dog. It had been treated as a clown and a coward, but there was something sinister about it. He had looked it up in the encyclopedia. A bull terrier. It had been bred in England for its fighting qualities. It had the strength of a bulldog and the quickness of a terrier. Courage, resistance to pain. The dogs were put in pits and fought to the death. Neat.

'Sure,' he said. 'Why not?'

His mother smiled, and for an instant he was afraid she might embrace him. He turned away. 'An *Englischer Hund. Sehr gut.* A *Schweinhund.*'

He went to a chair, slouched down into it, and looked at his mother. Her smile was gone, and her eyebrows were raised in exasperation. It was the expression he liked to see. It's the expression she likes to have, he thought. She's like me. He looked around the untidy room. She needs a junkyard; a bunker to crawl into. But adults can't do what they want to do. Carl was not eager to become an adult.

Two

John and Nancy Grafton drove the few blocks to the Fines' house in silence. They both glanced occasionally into the rear-view mirror, which John had adjusted to reflect the image of Baxter, who lay on the back seat, his eyes closed. Nancy wondered whether the dog sensed what was about to happen, and how it would react to having a new home.

John had not asked Nancy what she thought about giving Baxter away. He just announced that he had offered the dog to Jason Fine, and that the offer had been accepted. Nancy hadn't objected, and now they were pretending that there was nothing questionable about the act.

But when the car pulled up to the house Nancy was hesitant about getting out. She did not want to see the people who were going to shelter Baxter; who would look up from the newspaper to see him staring and would wonder what impulses lay behind the gaze.

'Aren't you coming in?' John asked.

'I'm not sure.'

'I want you to meet them,' John said. He put his hand on his wife's thigh. 'There won't be any problem. And then we'll be alone. We'll be alone in our house tonight.'

Nancy tried to imagine what that would be like. She had grown used to awakening in the middle of the night, immediately aware that Baxter lay somewhere near by. He's like a wart, she would think: something unattractive that one touches unconsciously in idle moments; something potentially dangerous.

She got out of the car and watched as John opened the back door. Baxter jumped to the ground and followed them cautiously to the house.

Jason Fine opened the door, smiled briefly at the couple, and then looked down at Baxter. His smile broadened. 'I thought you said it was a dog.'

John was relieved to see the smile. 'Actually, we lost the dog on the way over, so we brought you this instead. If you don't like it we'll take it back to the zoo.'

'We'll let Carl decide,' Jason said.

Carl was standing behind his father. Nancy watched the boy carefully as Baxter entered the house. Carl dropped to one knee and put a hand gently on the dog's head. It occurred to Nancy that neither she nor John had touched the dog since the baby died. Baxter's tail began to wag. Thank God, Nancy thought. There was an obvious rapport between the two. Let the animal have another chance.

How old was the boy? she wondered. Twelve, perhaps. Still a child, but uneasy with his childhood. Nancy had stopped looking at children. In the afternoon, when they played their mysterious games near her house, she turned on the television set, trying to ignore their energy and point-lessly dramatic screams.

But Carl was attractive: his uncared-for, smooth hands and soft hair. Would she ever have another child? It began to seem possible.

Sara Fine served them coffee. They spoke of the town and their lives, smiling at one another and glancing occasionally at Baxter and Carl. Everyone seemed pleased.

When Nancy and John left Baxter made no attempt to follow them, and the couple made no attempt to pretend regret. As the two families stood at the door Nancy said to Carl, 'You must be good to Baxter. That's very important.'

'I understand,' Carl said.

Sara Fine was puzzled by the seriousness with which

Nancy and Carl spoke. And later, when Carl took the dog out for a walk, she frowned slightly as she stood at the window and watched the boy and the dog move along the dark street. There was something remarkable about their immediate acceptance of each other. An uncommon friendship had begun.

2

I must be careful of the boy. He looks at me with an understanding I have never seen in the eyes of a human. He does not love me.

It is evening, and I am sitting tensely in the dining-room. The man and woman eat slowly, muttering frequently, and sometimes offering me a piece of their disgusting food. The boy glances at me occasionally. Soon he will get up from the table. He is as eager as I am to leave the house. This house is not as old as the others I have lived in. It has a feeling of impermanence and its odors are uninteresting; almost nothing in it smells of wood or earth. I have sensed no important traces of anyone except the boy, the man and the woman.

The boy gets up, but I do not move until he makes my sound. It is the same sound the others made when they wanted me to be near them. But there are other sounds the boy uses: one when he wants me to walk beside him; another when he wants me to sit still. When he taught me about the sounds he also taught me about pain. But he has also given me pleasure beyond anything I had known before. The pain is the price I paid for the pleasure. It is remarkable how strong the memory of pain is. I never hear those particular sounds he makes without feeling the chain tightening against my throat.

I wonder if it is the same with people; whether the sounds they are always making remind them of past pain. Probably not, or they would make fewer sounds.

Now the boy makes my sound, and we go out into the evening, hurrying to our pleasure. We pass between the two houses where I have caused pain. I wonder whether I will ever be forced to do so again. For, although the boy has taught me things in his crude way, I know—and I think he knows—that there are things he will learn from me.

3

Mary Cuzzo admired Carl Fine. Even today, on the last day of the semester, with the summer sun warm and dazzling in the tall-windowed classroom, he gave her his full attention. If Carl hadn't been in the room she might as well have been talking to herself. Some of her students were more subtly intelligent than Carl; some of them more aggressively charming. But Carl gave her his attention. Always. That was important to Miss Cuzzo.

She doesn't want us to leave, Carl thought. The other teachers had held shortened, informal classes. They were as eager as their students for the vacation to begin. Miss Cuzzo would spend the summer on Hawley Street with her father; sharing his discomfort.

The bell rang, and Carl moved his head slightly to look across the aisle, where Veronica Bartnik was sliding out from under her desk. She always showed Carl her thighs as she turned to get up. Because today was special she moved more slowly than usual to be certain that he would be able to glimpse the blue panties she had carefully chosen that morning. It was a tribute. Veronica usually paid little attention to boys her own age or younger. But she wanted to make a gesture to repay Carl's respectful interest. He had never spoken to her.

Carl was still seated when the rest of the class had left the room. He was immobilized with excitement. He thought of

Veronica, and of the summer that had now officially begun. He thought of the bunker.

Why is he waiting? Mary Cuzzo wondered. Does he have something to say to me?

'What are your plans for the summer, Carl?'

The boy looked up, startled. He had forgotten about the teacher. Before he could answer she was leaving the classroom. 'Enjoy yourself,' she said, without looking back.

Carl started after her, afraid he had been impolite. But he couldn't think of anything to say to her. Suddenly and inexplicably he was thinking of Baxter. He went down the quiet corridor and cleaned out his locker. He collected books, old sneakers, a scarf, and stuffed everything in a canvas bag—everything but a bundle of photographs, which he looked at carefully before tearing up. He dropped the pieces into a sewer on the way home.

Even before he entered his house, Carl heard the familiar, low-pitched scraping sound. It was one of the great irritations of his life that his mother played the cello. If she had to play an instrument why couldn't it be the piano or even the flute? He hated to see her sitting there with her legs spread and her eyes closed, struggling with the ungainly instrument. One of the reasons Carl never invited anyone to the house was that he wouldn't know how to explain it if they should discover his mother practicing.

Baxter met him at the door. There was no need to explain anything to Baxter. Carl crouched down and looked into the dog's small, deep-set eyes. He no longer heard the music. He thought about how easy it had been to train the dog. When he looked into its eyes he knew it was not a submissive animal. It obeyed him not out of fear, but out of understanding. There would be danger, he thought, in losing that understanding.

'My friend,' he said. 'Our summer has begun.'

Three

While the boy is inside his secret room I stand guard for him. I roam among the heaps of broken, unwanted objects, and I warn him when intruders are near. This territory is ours. I have marked every part of it with my scent, and I try especially to keep others of my kind away from us.

Am I different from those others? I believe so, but I cannot be sure, for there is no way of knowing the thoughts of another creature. There are many of us in the town. We do not look or smell alike, but there is one thing we have in common: a deep mistrust of one another. I suppose the reason most of us prefer human company to our own is simply that people are much less treacherous than we are.

But, as I said, I believe I am different from the others. I am not seeking mere security. I have learned that human trust can be uninteresting, and also that it can waver. I realize now, as I think the boy does, that one must accept one's nature.

I understand my own nature, but the nature of most humans puzzles me. What do they think when they see the littered territory where I now stand? Isn't their passion for collecting things diminished? Don't they realize that things are ultimately useless; that they must be discarded, leaving the people no better off than I am; I, who have never owned anything?

And yet, is it true that I have never owned anything? Don't I think of this territory as being mine, or at least mine and the boy's? Yes. I would fight to defend it. Am I being corrupted?

'You don't own me,' Veronica Bartnik said.

Her father stood in the doorway of her bedroom. 'Yes, I damn well do,' he said. 'And as long as I do, I'm not going to let you act like an animal.'

She's worse than an animal, he thought. Joseph Bartnik respected animals, for they had given him the only completely happy moments of his life; moments when he saw them across the sights of a rifle or a shotgun. During the hunting seasons he killed his limit or more, and during the rest of the year he cleaned his guns and felt uneasy.

Veronica watched her father. Shall I charm him? she wondered. She looked at his short, recently trimmed hair; his immaculate 'outdoorsman' clothes; the army boots he drunkenly polished every night. I understand why Mother left, she thought, but why didn't she take me with her? I can't be this man's daughter.

She smiled. 'You look nice,' she said.

He relaxed slightly. He knew she hadn't meant what she said, but a fight had been avoided. 'At least I'm clean,' he said. 'And now I want *you* to do some cleaning . . . yourself and your room. And then we're going out.'

'Where are we going?'

'To the junk-yard.'

'The *junk-yard*? Oh, Jesus, why?'

'Because I say so.'

He hates me, Veronica thought. He hates me because he owns me but can't use me. He only respects things he can use. The reason he always gave for going to the junk-yard was that 'there might be something there I can use'. He wasn't the only one who went to the junk-yard. There were others like him. Veronica watched them as she sat in the truck waiting for her father to finish poking about in the trash. Men and boys. Never any women. Boys too young or timid to be interested in girls; men who wanted to escape from women or who, like her father, had been abandoned by them. Theirs was a world without women, but it was not a masculine world. It was sexless.

Veronica's father left her room and went into the kitchen, where Queenie, his spaniel, was whining and clawing at the door. The dog was in heat. 'Poor bitch,' Mr. Bartnik said. 'You'll feel better soon.' It's like a sickness, he thought. He had refused to have her spayed, fearing it might affect her efficiency as a retriever.

He thought of the dawns they had spent together at the lake's edge, sharing excitement and discipline. Each year he feared the dog might forget its training and give in to its impulses. But it never failed him, sitting rigidly and silently until the first flights appeared, not flinching at the roar of the shotgun, not moving until his command; then diving into the cold water, swimming without hesitation, and returning, the bird held gently in strong jaws. Acting under the man's will rather than its own.

And now, in its heat, it showed no trace of discipline. It was aware only of its unselective need to couple. She's like all females, he thought. But at least with a dog it was a temporary condition. Joseph Bartnik watched females carefully and with disapproval. He disapproved of the interest they took in shelter and in their own bodies. They've never come out of the caves, he thought. Women's liberation. You might as well try to liberate a turtle; what else could it possibly become?

What you do, if they are yours, is protect them from themselves. He attached the chain leash to Queenie's collar and went out to the pickup truck to wait for Veronica. On his way he looked into the mailbox. It was an act he performed hesitantly. Even now, after three years, he still vaguely expected to find an envelope with his wife's childish handwriting; still expecting an explanation.

3

Carl Fine's bunker had become surprisingly comfortable —too comfortable, he sometimes thought. Even under the sun of cloudless afternoons, when the metal of wrecked cars was too hot to touch, the bunker was pleasantly cool. Carl had spent hours carefully arranging the framework of his refuge. He placed light-colored metals on the roof to reflect the sun; he enlarged and deepened the inner chamber. Complex channels were arranged for ventilation, and a large, shielded piece of transparent plastic gave the chamber a soft illumination in the daytime.

Carl was seldom able to relax in the daytime, however. Summer idleness and boredom drew intruders to the junkyard every day, and the weekends were periods of siege. On Saturday afternoons Carl never entered the bunker, but wandered its perimeter while Baxter ranged through the area, barking alarms as each new trespasser arrived.

It was on a Saturday that Mr. Bartnik appeared. Carl heard the truck pull up and wondered why Baxter had not barked. The boy walked to the top of a mound of trash. Baxter stood at the side of the truck, moving silently back and forth, his ears flattened against his head. Carl had never seen him look so confused or uncertain. Then Mr. Bartnik opened the door of the pickup, and a brown, curly-haired dog leaped to the ground, straining against its leash.

Baxter rushed to the other dog and buried his nose under its tail. Mr. Bartnik got out of the truck and kicked Baxter, who didn't raise his head, and hardly seemed to notice the attack. Mr. Bartnik pulled on his dog's leash and kicked at Baxter again.

Carl ran towards the man and shouted, 'Stop that.'

Mr. Bartnik stopped, his foot pulled back, his boot glinting in the sunlight. 'Is this your mutt?' he said.

'That's my dog.'

'Then call him off.'

My dog, thought Carl. It was the first time he had used those words, and they pleased him. He stumbled his way to Baxter and pulled him from the other dog. Mr. Bartnik picked up his spaniel, pushed it into the cab of the pickup, and slammed the door. It was then that Carl saw Veronica. She was smiling at him.

Veronica's father said, 'You shouldn't let your dog run loose like that.'

'He didn't do anything.'

'He was about to.'

'You didn't have to kick him,' Carl said.

Baxter was pulling towards the truck door, still seemingly unaware of anything except the other dog. Carl was disappointed. Why hadn't Baxter fought the man?

Veronica said, 'Hello, Carl.'

Her father said, 'Don't let Queenie out.'

Queenie, Carl thought. A sissy name. He wondered how long the dog would last in a fight with Baxter. Queenie. Carl looked at Veronica. He was too upset to be embarrassed by her unexpected friendliness.

Mr. Bartnik was staring at Carl and Baxter. Both of them had forgotten him. They're randy, he thought. Stupid and randy. Both of them were entranced, as though they had come across a treasure while poking through the trash. The man put his hand on Carl's thin shoulder. 'That's my daughter and my dog,' he said.

'It's all right, Daddy,' Veronica said. 'This is Carl Fine. He was in my class at school.'

Mr. Bartnik frowned and turned to look across the junkyard. Bits of glass glittered in the sunlight. He became aware of the silence; the inert, random materials.

'You stay in the truck,' he said to his daughter, and walked away from her; away from the town.

Veronica was staring at Carl. It was hot in the truck, and she could feel sweat beginning to accumulate under her arms, between her breasts and buttocks. The dogs whined.

'You know who you look like?' Carl asked her.

I've underestimated him, Veronica thought. Nothing interested her more than her own appearance. She had looked at herself more carefully than she had ever looked at anything else. She knew her eyelashes, her toenails, each passing blemish of her skin, and yet she was puzzled by the uniqueness of what she saw. She knew she had an attractiveness, but she wanted to have beauty. To her that meant she should look like someone else. True beauty, she believed, was an ideal that everyone recognized and admired. Grace Kelly, for example. Princess Grace. If you didn't resemble a great beauty, you weren't truly beautiful.

'Who do I look like?' she asked.

'Eva Braun.'

'Eva Braun? Who the hell is Eva Braun?'

'She was Adolf Hitler's mistress.'

'Very funny,' Veronica said. What a dumb thing to say, she thought. She didn't know much about Hitler. A silly-looking madman. He couldn't have attracted a beautiful woman.

'I'm serious,' Carl said. He took a creased photograph from his pocket and handed it to her.

Veronica studied it carefully. The image was not clear. A blonde woman or girl—it was hard to guess her age—wearing some kind of peasant costume. It looked like an illustration for a fairy tale. Gretel in *Hansel and Gretel*, maybe. She might have been beautiful, but it was a strange beauty. Innocent.

'She doesn't look like anyone's mistress,' Veronica said.

'They got married in the end. Then they killed themselves. If it had been anyone but Hitler, people would have thought it was a great love story.'

Veronica didn't like love stories. Not any more. It was hard for her to believe that two years ago she had read and reread *Little Women*, and had wept when Jo fell in love. Then she had discovered the books and photographs that her father kept on the top shelf of his closet. And later, when she found herself on a blanket in the back of Frank Alio's station wagon, it didn't occur to her to wonder whether she was in love with him. She only wondered whether they would feel the kind of excitement the people in her father's books felt; whether they would look the way the people looked in the photographs.

She looked again at the picture of Eva Braun. 'Do you think she's beautiful?' she asked Carl.

'Yes,' Carl said, and then blushed, realizing he had just implied that he thought Veronica was beautiful. Suddenly he was uncomfortable. The sun was hot on his shoulders. Baxter was whimpering and standing with his front legs against the truck's door. Carl felt very young. 'I'd better go before your father gets back,' he said.

Veronica refolded the picture, but instead of handing it back to him she put it in her canvas shoulder-bag. Carl started to protest, but then realized he wanted her to have it.

'Do you come here often?' Veronica asked.

'Yes. Baxter likes it here.'

'Baxter?'

'My dog.'

Veronica smiled for a moment and then said, 'I think Queenie likes it here, too. I have to walk her every night. Maybe I should bring her here some time.'

Carl felt his hands begin to tremble. He leaned over and took Baxter's collar and pulled the dog away from the truck. He couldn't look at the girl. 'I'll see you,' he said as he moved away from her, pulling clumsily at Baxter.

Veronica could see her father walking back towards the truck. His hands were empty. As he approached she said, 'Didn't you find anything?'

'Nothing worth picking up,' he said.

In his pocket was a torn, soiled pair of panty hose.

4

Mary Cuzzo and her father sat on their front porch, the afternoon heat enveloping them. They were bored and impatient, as though they were in a theater waiting to see a performance that should have begun thirty minutes earlier.

Mary would have preferred to be inside the house, working on her card file, but the old man liked to have her near him as he watched the movements of their neighbors. He didn't expect her to talk, though, and she was grateful for that. When school was in session she had to talk incessantly and, it seemed to her, futilely. The summer was better. Ironically, it was easier for her to ignore the emptiness of her own life when she wasn't forced to be with the young.

At school it was difficult to believe that the energy and enthusiasms of her students would not lead them to pleasures and satisfactions she had missed. But in the quiet of her house she was able to gain perspective, to see the truth. This summer she had begun to keep a card file: one card for every student she had taught in the past sixteen years. On each card she had placed two categories of entries: facts and conclusions. The facts were random and varied: went to college; bathed infrequently; alcoholic; had two children; suffered nosebleeds; had abortion; drove truck; deceased. The conclusions, with few exceptions, were uniform: unhappy; early promise unfulfilled.

There were many students she had lost track of: those who had left town and never returned, who never wrote to those still here. But she had no reason to think they might be any more successful or happy than those who stayed. Was it the town that corrupted them? she wondered. Were they an unfortunate, unrepresentative generation? No. Their parents were no different.

She heard a whistling from down the street. Bach. One of the suites for unaccompanied cello. Carl Fine. He would have learned the melody from his mother. Miss Cuzzo wondered what entries she would have on Carl's card in ten years. Would he be one of the exceptions? If not, what would contaminate his life?

As he passed Carl smiled at her and waved. Mary went into the house and wrote on his card: 'Has dog.'

Four

Perhaps the boy thinks I have gone mad. Can he understand any more than I do how a bitch's scent could reduce me to a state of helplessness? I think about those disgusting minutes; about the bitch's ridiculous mud-toned coat, and I want to destroy her. Yet I know if I were with her now my anger would be swept away, and I would want only to mount her.

Do humans know this kind of desire? Maybe some of them do. I think of the young couple who left their child unprotected to go to their bedroom. And the scent that women —even the old woman—have about them constantly; a scent reminiscent of the one the bitch has. Such a thing would explain the instability of people. But it cannot be. Constant sexual temptation would be intolerable. One would be overcome with shame at one's helplessness.

I don't think the boy feels shame. It is one of his many virtues. Most humans have few virtues. But, of course, they have many disadvantages to overcome. Their peculiar bodies, for example. Tall creatures that walk on two legs must be in a constant state of anxiety. The ground is a threat to them. They build furniture. It is ridiculous to avoid the element that supports you.

The only admirable part of the human body, I think, is the hand. I have seen it do the most delicate things: the old woman making patterns with dark and light threads, pushing a needle through tiny crevices. And I have felt the strength of hands. But people obviously misuse their hands. I see the discarded materials in the place where the boy and I go. I think of the dexterity and strength of the hands that made the objects, and I realize that the effort was wasted. The hands must be kept busy; activities must be invented.

The boy's mother is an example. She sits for hours with her instrument, her left hand touching the strings quickly and firmly. I lie in the corner and listen to the sounds she produces: complex sounds that are low enough to make the floor vibrate and yet have a barely audible high-pitched edge to them. She is one of the rare people who seems interested in sounds other than monotonous chatter.

And yet her sounds have no meaning. They are less interesting than the random sounds of real life that fill the neighborhood: a raised voice; footsteps; a slamming door.

The boy realizes that truth. He knows the whining of the bitch in the automobile was more meaningful than the sound of any instrument. He saw me undone by the dark, squealing creature. He does not know about my strength and cleverness. He does not know about my triumphs. I must show him that I too have uncommon virtues.

2

Sara Fine wondered what Baxter was thinking. The dog was obviously interested in the music. He was the only one who enjoyed being in the house when she was practicing. Is it just another noise to him? Without pausing, she interrupted the Bach she was playing and began to produce random, patternless tones. The dog showed no awareness of the change in the music. It was only when Sara played a series of high harmonics that he lifted his head slightly.

Her son came into the room, his hands over his ears, his eyes rolling. 'All right,' he shouted. 'I'll eat my broccoli. I'll mow the lawn. Anything. Just . . .' He dropped to his knees. 'Just have mercy.'

Baxter began to bark.

Sara put aside her bow. She smiled, but she was uneasy. She felt, as she often did, a nasty undercurrent in Carl's playfulness. 'It was an experiment,' she said.

'It failed, my dear.'

Carl had taken to calling his mother 'my dear'. It was added to his repertory: the Frankenstein monster walk, the word 'boring' and his Nazi routine. What did it all conceal, Sara wondered. Adolescents constructed their surfaces so energetically, so elaborately. It was an attempt to disguise what they were discovering about themselves. Sara was more comfortable with younger children, who had no disguises, or with adults, whose masks were more easily penetrated.

Sara went into the kitchen, leaving Carl and the dog to their undecipherable thoughts and feelings. Had the dog changed the boy? They were inseparable. Carl had taken on an affection and a responsibility, but Sara was not sure there was virtue in that alone. Yet she supposed there was little chance of either one corrupting the other. Without words the possibilities for corruption are small.

Carl was lying on the rug, his face close to Baxter's. I wish we could talk to each other, he thought.

'You'd like to screw old Bartnik's spaniel, wouldn't you?' he whispered.

Baxter's tail wagged.

It's so easy for you, the boy thought. Nothing to learn, nothing to be afraid of. No wondering what to say, no embarrassment. Why can't we all be animals? Why can't we be ourselves? I'm learning to be myself, Carl thought. Baxter is teaching me. Until recently Carl had been resigned to a life of docile confusion. He did what his parents and teachers asked of him, but what they asked made no sense to him. He obeyed because he realized that there must be order. There were young people in the town who resisted order, and for a time he had admired them. He had stood beside John Terrel in the school yard, watching him remove the money from a stolen purse. He had watched from the shadows as stones were thrown through school windows. Those who did these things sensed he was not one of them, but they accepted him as what he was: an uncritical observer.

But he knew he was different from them just as he was different from those who comfortably followed the rules. Slowly he began to realize that it wasn't necessary to join either group; that he might establish his own order, based on his own nature. But first he had to explore that nature. And so he began to spend the hours in the bunker. And he watched Baxter, who lived comfortably in a system that was alien to his nature, and who was admired and trusted.

Carl put his hand on Baxter's white head. Time and discipline, he thought. Those are the important things. I have time; I'm not a man yet. And discipline is easy for me. But there is something else, something in my nature I don't yet recognize.

At Baxter's side was a long, slender bone the dog had found in the junk-yard and had carried back to the house. He spent hours chewing on it, sometimes growling softly. Carl reached for the bone, and the dog immediately grasped one end of it between his teeth. Carl got to his knees and tried to pull the bone from the dog's jaws. It was a game they played often. It was a game Carl had never won.

3

Nancy Grafton heard the familiar whistling. She left the kitchen and went to the front door. She pulled the curtain aside slightly and watched as Carl and Baxter hurried past the house. Did the dog glance at her? Or had he forgotten the events that he still brought vividly to her mind?

She looked at the Prescott house across the street. It was still empty. There had been a period when the real estate agent brought people to see the property. Nancy had watched eagerly as couples and families entered the house. She wanted them to like it. But they emerged dull-eyed and obviously eager to be somewhere else. No one came to the house now.

Nancy tried to remember what had seemed so attractive to her when she and John had first driven down the block. She wasn't sure now. But she wasn't ready to leave the town. Even though she no longer loved it, she did not want it to die.

As Nancy turned to go back into the kitchen a young blonde girl passed the house. The girl was pulling hard against a leash, trying to restrain a brown dog that seemed not to notice the pressure of the collar against its throat.

The girl was about Carl's age. If the town were to be saved it would be by those like Carl and the girl. Nancy imagined them together in the Prescott house, bringing it their life and simplicity.

4

It was dusk. Carl sat beside the bunker, looking across the shadowy, jagged landscape of the junk-yard. The high-pitched sounds of night had begun: crickets; frogs in the nearby pond; roosting birds. He also heard an occasional whine from within the bunker, where he had barricaded Baxter.

The boy looked towards the town. Lights were being turned on; cars moved through the streets. He wondered why more people weren't outdoors. They're like snails, he thought. They need the shells of their houses and automobiles. Not as much for shelter as for reassurance. I don't need the shell, he thought. I've cast myself out.

A silhouette was moving toward him, fading and reappearing against the uneven light of the background. He knew it was Veronica before he could see her features. He recognized the outline of her body; her way of moving. She dropped Queenie's leash, and the spaniel ran ahead of her, straight to Carl, jumping against him and barking. Baxter was also barking now, and pushing against the door of the bunker. Carl squatted, running his hand through Queenie's curly coat, but not taking his eyes off the girl's approaching figure.

'Veronica?' he said.

'Is it you, Carl?'

'Yes.' Carl was unhappily aware of the high pitch of his voice.

'Is Baxter there?'

'He's in the bunker.'

'The what?'

Veronica had stopped a few feet away.

'The bunker,' Carl said. 'A sort of cave I built.'

'What do you want with a cave?'

'I take cave women there,' Carl said.

Oh God, he thought, what am I saying? He had decided that if Veronica showed up he would let her decide what they would say and do. He knew that in his nervousness he could only create an atmosphere of silliness. Would she think he was an idiot?

Veronica smiled. He's terrified, she thought. It was reassuring. With older boys, she was usually the uncomfortable one. 'Do you know many cave women?' she asked.

'None. Actually, the bunker is just in case I meet one.'

'Why do you call it a bunker?'

'Hitler lived in a bunker. At the end of the war.'

'With Eva Braun?"

'Yes. And they had a dog called Blondie. The dog had four puppies there.' Carl was beginning to lose his self-consciousness. The story of Hitler's last days moved him more than anything else he knew about, and it was the first time he had told the story to anyone. 'Hitler loved Blondie. And he carried one of the puppies around with him—petting it all the time. He had these cyanide capsules he was going to use to kill himself and Eva. But he wasn't sure they would work—he didn't trust the people that gave them to him. So he gave one to Blondie. He watched her die. And then he had the puppies shot.'

'That's disgusting,' Veronica said.

'No. He loved them. Here's the really great part. He left instructions. After he and Eva were dead—she took a capsule, and he shot himself in the head—they were cremated. And so were Blondie and the puppies. And all the ashes were mixed together.'

Carl became silent. Queenie moved nervously about, avoiding the bunker, where Baxter was clawing at the metal door.

Veronica looked at Carl. He's forgotten me, she thought. She wasn't used to being ignored by boys, especially by one who was alone with her in the dark. She was flattered. Carl had shared a secret with her. 'Why don't you let Baxter out?' she asked.

Carl walked to the bunker and pulled the door aside. Baxter sprang out of the darkness and then stood motionless. Queenie stopped prowling, and the dogs stared at each other briefly. Then Baxter charged at Queenie, who growled and retreated towards Veronica.

'It's all right,' the girl said, and took hold of Queenie's leash.

Baxter approached more cautiously now, moving behind Queenie, sniffing intently. The spaniel growled again and snapped, turning to keep her head towards Baxter. The dogs stared at each other for perhaps a minute. Then Baxter leaped forward and in one motion grasped Queenie's throat in his mouth.

Carl started to lean over and pull the dogs apart, but then he realized that Baxter was not using his full strength. Queenie yelped and struggled briefly. When she stopped Baxter moved quickly to mount her. Queenie no longer resisted.

Veronica took Carl's hand and held it tightly. There's no joy in it, she thought. Queenie stared out into the darkness. Baxter's body jerked hideously and convulsively. It was not what the girl had expected, and it did not end quickly. When it was over she immediately led Queenie away, towards the town.

Carl started after them, but stumbled and fell. His legs were shaking. He wanted to call out to Veronica; to thank her. But there was a tightness in his throat. He had never before been so happy.

Five

I should have killed the bitch. Not before the act; that would have been impossible. But after, when my humiliation was ended; when we were separated, standing foolishly before the boy and girl. The bitch was sickening to me then: her odor; her ugly coat; her passivity. Yet I could not harm her. Why?

I suppose I pitied her. And it was obvious that what happened had not been her will. It had been as unpleasant for her as it had been for me. As the girl led her away there was a moment when I felt what seemed to be a sort of affection. But it must have been pity. In any case, I showed compassion, and that was a mistake. Weakness is always a mistake.

We are passing the couple's house. I think of how often they used to perform the act. They seemed to enjoy it, but I realize now how unpleasant it must have been for them. And I begin to pity them too.

I must be more careful. Pity is not an emotion I want to encourage in myself. It is something for humans to feel; one of the jumble of odd sentiments they burden themselves with. Their emotions are like diseases, I think; diseases that can spread among those who try to understand them.

Let their feelings be a mystery, like the dozens of other strange traits they have. They live too far from reality. They stare at the television set as if it were something real and not just a jumble of noisy shadows. I suppose even those shadows inspire emotions in them.

The ways they have to deceive themselves are endless.

Carl's parents were seated at either end of the sofa, watching television. Or, rather, the television set was on. The program was a rerun of a show they had watched and been bored by months before. Jason Fine glanced at his wife. She was staring at the carpet, her expression unsettled, as though she had seen movement in a plate of food. The expression was a familiar one to Jason, and there had been a period when he had found it alarming. But now it comforted him.

The darkness of Sara's vision had been merely exciting for him in the beginning, but it had gradually become a necessity. The women he knew before Sara had tended to treat him as they would treat a friendly dog. They appreciated his uncomplicated affection, and they sometimes returned it, but in an absent-minded way. Sara had honored him with her ruefulness.

They lived quietly, seldom touching, making few friends in the town. Jason returned gratefully to the untidy house each night as though it were a secret clubhouse. He talked and Sara listened; her silence lending an unsuspected significance to the events he described. She pleased him.

The only mistake in their marriage had been the birth of their son. Carl was an intruder neither of them understood. Jason sometimes wished he could keep the boy in his office. He could deal with him there; could smile and talk with him as he did with the others.

Jason looked at his wife again. She turned to look at him. She didn't smile, but her features softened, and she gave him her full attention. I love her, he thought. Perhaps if I didn't I would be closer to the boy. Perhaps I would be wondering where he is now, and would resent the amount of time he spends away from the house. But instead I am grateful for his absence.

Jason got up and switched the television set off. Instead of returning to the couch he sat in a chair facing his wife. 'Shall I tell you a story?' he asked.

Since Carl's birth, their lovemaking had changed drastically. They had never returned to the more or less conventional sex life of their early marriage. Instead Jason would speak to Sara: improvizing, fantasizing. And they would touch themselves as he spoke, linked only by his words and the sight of each other. The game never failed to gratify them, and it never occurred to either of them that there was anything less than beautiful about it.

'Carl will be home soon,' Sara said.

'I suppose so,' Jason said. 'Are you still worried about him?'

'Not worried, exactly. Just puzzled. Although I don't know why I should be. Carl's a lot like I am, I suppose.'

Jason didn't comment. He didn't think the boy was like either of them.

Sara continued: 'There's one big difference, though. He has no obvious obsession . . . nothing like my music, I mean.'

'Does everyone have to have an obsession?'

'Certainly. It's your choice of one that determines whether you're sane or not.'

'What's my obsession?' Jason asked.

'I am, of course.'

'Does that qualify me for sanity?'

'Just barely. You picked an acceptable category, but you chose badly within it.'

Jason let the remark go. He knew Sara would not want him to deny it. 'Then I was insane before I met you?'

'No. You had your baseball players.'

Jason blushed. From the time he was Carl's age until his marriage he had kept a file of index cards on which he

84

recorded the height and weight of every active baseball player in the major leagues. He had never seen a professional game except on television, and he had only played a few softball games himself. It was all incredible to him now; the years of research and correspondence. Maybe he *had* been insane.

He had told Sara about the collection the first time he went out with her. She had not commented. She merely looked at him ambiguously for a moment and changed the subject. The next night he loaded the boxes of cards into his car and drove to the junk-yard. He stacked the boxes on the ground and started to light a match. But he put the matches back in his pocket, got in the car, and drove away.

Neither of them had ever mentioned the cards again, and he assumed Sara had forgotten about them.

Sara was looking at him fondly. 'All right?' she said. They were the words she always used instead of 'I'm sorry'.

'All right,' Jason said. And he changed the subject: 'John Grafton asked me again today how we're getting along with Baxter. I think they must miss him.'

'Maybe we should ask them over for dinner some time,' Sara said. She remembered the day the Graftons delivered Baxter to the house. There was a pensiveness about them, combined with a suppressed energy, that she found attractive. They would be polite and slightly uncomfortable during dinner. And they probably would not return the invitation. They were the kind of guests Sara liked.

Jason was surprised. Sara hardly ever suggested that sort of thing. She let her husband plan their social life, usually agreeing to his suggestions, but without enthusiasm. 'That might be nice,' he said. 'Why don't you call Nancy and arrange it?'

The front door opened, and Carl and Baxter appeared. The dog went into the kitchen and began to lap noisily from his water dish. Carl greeted his parents by raising his eyebrows a few times in what he thought was a reasonable imitation of Groucho Marx. 'Nothing on television?' he asked.

'Nothing exciting,' his father said. 'I think they're running out of Helmut Dantine movies.'

'The *Schweins*,' Carl said.

It was obvious to Sara and Jason that despite the boy's efforts to be casual, he was in a state of excitement and confusion. He switched on the television set and sat on the floor, his back against the sofa.

Carl and his parents stared at the screen, all of them unseeing.

Baxter lay under the kitchen table. For the first time since he had been in the house he would not sleep in Carl's room.

3

Veronica Bartnik's father was sitting at the kitchen table. His back was straight, but his head moved erratically when he tried to look at his daughter. In front of him were a bottle of Scotch and the kind of glass that cheese spreads are sold in.

'Where've you been?' he asked.

'Walking the dog.'

'A long walk.'

Veronica didn't bother to answer. There was a time when her father had kept the whisky bottle hidden. It had been better then. He should pretend he didn't drink, just as she was pretending she had done nothing but walk the dog.

Veronica went to her bedroom. Queenie followed her and lay down in a corner.

'I'm sorry,' the girl said.

We should protect them, she thought. It's not as if they were wild. They depend on us. She squatted next to the dog and began to scratch its head. 'We won't go back to that place,' she said.

4

Carl sat on a discarded clothes-dryer, staring through the dusk towards the town. He was intensely aware of his body, which was exceptionally tired and clean. He had slept only an hour or two the previous night, and he had bathed carefully before dinner, chafing parts of his body with the small brush his father used to scrub his fingernails.

A candle burned in the bunker.

They should be here soon. As he lay awake the previous night Carl had imagined the arrival of the girl and the dog dozens of times. He had invented conversations and scenarios, all of which ended with him and Veronica lying together in the bunker. One of the few possibilities he had not considered was that the girl would not appear.

As the darkness increased, and the truth became apparent to him, he became conscious of his isolation. It was one of the few times—perhaps the only time—he could remember wanting not to be alone.

It's a mistake to depend on another person, he thought; wrong to need someone. Baxter trotted up to him and sat panting. He had been running hard, probably chasing a stray mongrel away. The dog doesn't need anyone, Carl thought. He uses us, as he used Veronica's spaniel, but he doesn't need us. There were stories about dogs that languished and starved at an owner's grave. But Baxter hadn't shown any remorse at leaving his previous owners . . . no more than he would show if he had to leave me, Carl thought. I can learn more from him than from Veronica.

Baxter was suddenly standing and growling. Barely visible ahead of them was a large, emaciated brown-and-white dog. Its long coat was stained and matted. It stood its ground calmly as Baxter growled again and moved towards it.

Most of the strays in town had been made spiritless by months or years of begging and scavenging. Baxter tolerated them in the junk-yard unless they moved too close to the bunker, then he would rim them off. There was nothing abject about the dog that faced them now. It had an obvious strength in its lean body, and its gaze was steady.

Carl had never seen Baxter challenged before.

The dogs were motionless for a few seconds, and then Baxter moved cautiously towards the mongrel, who stood at the top of a pile of rubbish. Baxter made a short charge, but stopped before any contact was made. His opponent crouched tensely but did not retreat.

Baxter, who was at a disadvantage in having to attack from low ground, began to circle the other dog, stopping occasionally to reverse his field. The mongrel pivoted carefully but did not retreat, even when Baxter began to make a series of quick feints and lunges, nipping the larger dog occasionally.

It was obvious now that the challenge to Baxter was totally serious. The stray was not inviting a simple test of nerve; its intentions were deadly. Baxter rested for a moment, considering his opponent, and then turned almost casually and began to walk away.

He's a coward, Carl thought. The boy felt his jaw slacken. He realized he had been biting his lower lip in excitement. Now he began to think of his own safety. Perhaps the mongrel would come after him. He was about to look for something he could defend himself with when the stray charged at the retreating Baxter.

Carl wanted to call out a warning, but the action was too quick. The instant the attack began Baxter dropped to the ground, rolling on to his back and opening his jaws. The mongrel's momentum carried him directly over Baxter's waiting jaws, which closed viciously and surely on his throat. The muscles in Baxter's thick chest distended, and the other dog's growl became a whine. Then there was the snapping of bone and cartilage. Baxter was on his feet, his jaws still gripping the now grotesquely twisted neck. He stood for a moment, supporting the limp form. Then he loosened his grip and allowed the body to collapse. He circled it several times, watching cautiously at first, but eventually moving closer and sniffing intently. Then, looking up at Carl, Baxter lifted his right hind leg. Urine squirted over the lifeless form of the mongrel, rolling off its greasy coat, and darkening the earth.

Carl had forgotten Veronica. The desire that had earlier seemed of incomparable importance had vanished. And he realized that there were experiences more meaningful than sex. He went to the bunker and called to Baxter. They lay side by side in the guttering light of the candle. The boy ran his hand over the dog's body, which seemed to be sound and unmarked.

'You enjoyed it, didn't you?' Carl said. And then he reached for his box of magazine clippings. He passed over those of Eva, and picked out one of the man who had brought death to her; the man who had brought death to many.

Six

Do humans ever attack one another? If attacked, would they have the courage to do what I have done? I doubt it. I doubt whether they have a true understanding of death and violence. Death is not something they use, but something that uses them. They absorb themselves in their strange, acquisitive pursuits, smiling and muttering, never knowing the exhilaration that comes with the ultimate activity. They live too long, I think; they get too used to life.

The boy is truly mine now. He looks at me with a new esteem, and his touch has become cautious. He knows that I could do to him what I did to the animal that was foolish enough to challenge me. He knows that if we were to confront each other he would become my victim, despite his size and his skillful hands. He knows my nature.

Many people in the town know me now. They don't understand me the way the boy and the young couple do, but I can sense their respect for me. I notice how they stare into my eyes and move aside almost imperceptibly as I pass them on the street. They do not lean over and touch me condescendingly as I see them do with others of my kind.

It is harder to gain the respect of humans than it is to gain their love, and I sometimes feel pride in having won the regard of so many. I have done it on my own terms, by establishing my natural superiority rather than by fawning on them.

Occasionally I even feel a fondness for them.

It's like a morgue, Nancy Grafton thought. She was pushing a shopping cart past the meat section of the large supermarket that had recently opened at the edge of the town. She had begun to shiver as soon as she entered the market. The refrigerated air and the blue fluorescent light contrasted violently with the hot summery haze outside. The store was almost deserted.

She had never felt comfortable in supermarkets. She resented not knowing who might be on the other side of the tall, isolating displays. The situation reminded her of something that had frightened her as a child . . . had it been a story she read or a nightmare? She or another girl was in a maze with a wild animal. She walked for hours in terror, knowing the animal was near, but not knowing whether it was approaching her from behind or whether it would be waiting for her around the next corner.

She rolled her cart silently through the aisles. White-coated stock clerks passed her. The symmetrical rows of merchandise and the background whine of refrigeration machinery unsettled her. When she reached the meat displays her stomach tightened, and she turned away. She went back towards the entrance, taking the few articles she had in her cart and replacing them on the shelves.

'Nancy?'

It was Sara Fine. Nancy forced herself to smile, but her panic increased. She tried to concentrate. Sara seemed tense. Her usual air of pleasant disinterest, which Nancy admired, was missing.

She wants to talk, Nancy thought. Please don't let her mention the dog. Not now. She stared at Sara, trying not to hear her, and answering her questions absently.

'Yes, John's all right.'

I want to be like you when I'm your age; heavier and plainer than I need be. Careless of myself.

'Dinner?'

Anything. Just let me go now.

'Next Thursday should be fine. I'll check with John and let you know.'

If it weren't for the dog, we could be friends.

'I'm sorry, I have to run now.'

I'll be safe in a minute.

As Nancy started away Sara said, 'Baxter's eating habits aren't helping our food bill.' She reached into her cart and pulled out a plastic-wrapped package of liver. Blood leaked out of the package and dribbled down Sara's fingers.

Before Nancy reached her car she was weeping.

3

Carl moved a battered television set into place, closing the circular wall he had built around the pit. He wondered if the wall was high enough. Baxter, who had been lying in the pit, stood up as the boy climbed out.

Carl stood at the rim of the pit and called the dog. Baxter hesitated briefly and then tried to scramble up the wall. His forelegs reached the edge of the pit, but he lost his hold and fell back. He got to his feet again and moved in a circle, examining the walls of the structure. At one point two small wooden crates were stacked up unevenly, in a step-like arrangement. Baxter ran to the boxes and bounded easily out of the pit.

Carl wondered whether it was fair to have an escape route. Yes, he decided. The purpose of the pit was to allow a test of courage, not to make a death inevitable. It looked as though it would serve its purpose. They would know soon

. . . as soon as an opponent could be forced or enticed into the pit with Baxter. Tonight, perhaps.

Thunder sounded in the distance. Carl had seen no lightning, but a black, vertical cloud had appeared beyond the town. The air was moist and still. The boy started home, Baxter following him.

By the time they reached Hawley Street a strong, erratic wind was penetrating the densely packed leaves of the elms. Lightning struck, close enough for its flash and the sizzling crack of thunder to be simultaneous. Carl ran to the shelter of the nearest porch. It was the still empty Prescott house. Baxter hesitated, and then joined the boy. The rain hissed and splashed along the dark street. Carl sat on the glider and watched as lights appeared in some of the houses.

Dimly, through the rain, he saw Nancy Grafton standing in her doorway. She was beautiful. He had been strongly aware of that when she and her husband delivered Baxter, and now in the strange light he thought she was the most attractive person he had ever seen. She seemed to be made of light. Yet he remembered how substantial her breasts had been under her blouse that day.

How old was she? In her early twenties, probably. Not old enough to have forgotten what it was like to be his age, yet old enough to have outgrown the self-concern of someone like Veronica Bartnik. She left the doorway. The rain continued.

Baxter moved nervously about the porch.

Carl got up and looked behind him at the dirt-greyed windows of the old house. One of them was open slightly. He raised it and peered inside. The house was still furnished.

'Shall we go in?' he said to Baxter.

The dog had moved away from him, to the edge of the steps. Carl looked at the houses across the street. No one seemed to be looking out of windows; no one would see him go into the house. He picked up Baxter and carried him to the window. The dog resisted and jumped out of his arms, back to the porch.

'All right. Stay there.'

Dust rose from the sofa as Carl climbed over it into the musty gloom of the parlor. Lightning struck again, and the room was harshly illuminated for an instant, as by a photographer's flashgun. In that instant Carl was frightened, but his fear immediately turned to a pleasureful excitement. He had often wondered what the interiors of these old houses were like. So different from his own house. The space and the shadows.

He began to feel some of the ill-defined satisfaction he always felt in the isolation of the bunker. He walked slowly across the room, and then stopped as he saw movement at the landing of the staircase. Lightning flashed once more, and a gust of cool, damp air moved past him. He saw the movement again; something pale. His fear returned. This is where the woman had died. He remembered now. She had fallen.

He forced himself to move to the foot of the stairway. And then he realized what he saw was the dusty white curtain at the landing window moving in the draft. He continued up the stairs, the boards creaking beneath his feet.

He felt his way along the dark hall, opening doors as he came to them. The bathroom: a wide-edged, marble washbasin; an enormous claw-footed tub; an overhead toilet tank with a chain. He felt an urge to urinate. He moved to the toilet and pulled down the zipper on his jeans. But as he put his hand into his shorts he discovered that the urge he felt was sexual. He stood for a moment, feeling the stiffness grow beneath his hand.

'No,' he said aloud. 'Not now. Not this time.' He left the room.

He found three bedrooms. In two of them the closets were empty, the beds without linen. In the third he found some of Mrs. Prescott's clothes and several sheets in a dresser drawer. He put a sheet on the bed and lay down. The rain was slackening. After a few minutes he got up and went to the window. Across the street, on the second floor of the Grafton house, Nancy was turning her bedroom light out. Just before the room went dark he saw the indistinct but unmistakable outline of her nude body.

And then Baxter began to bark.

'Damn,' Carl said.

The barking became continuous, mingling with the rumble of distant thunder. Carl ran downstairs to the open window, where Baxter stood on his hind legs, looking into the house.

'Be quiet,' Carl said. 'I'll be out in a minute.'

He closed the window and started towards the back of the house. As he passed the fireplace he paused. There was one framed photograph on the mantel: a photograph of Mrs. Prescott and what could only have been Baxter. Carl put the picture into his pocket and went through the kitchen to the back door. There was a key in the lock. Carl left the house, locking the door behind him and putting the key in his pocket. He called Baxter, and they went through the back yard and started home through the alley.

As they walked Carl took out the photograph. Baxter had belonged to the old woman. No one had told him that. The woman had died.

The boy looked at the picture. Baxter standing; his fore-legs pushing against the old woman's frail thigh. The dog was obviously the stronger of the two.

Raindrops splashed against the glass that covered the photograph, diffusing and distorting the image.

Carl looked up and saw Baxter running ahead of him sniffing at trash cans.

'My God,' the boy said. 'You did it.'

And what about the death of the Graftons' child? Baxter

had been responsible for that too. That's why they wanted to get rid of him. And now he's mine. He does my bidding. Carl was smiling.

4

Mary Cuzzo listened regretfully to the receding thunder. She had always enjoyed storms. One of her most vivid early memories was of being in a car with her father and watching the dark, unstable funnel of a tornado move across the horizon. It was the most beautiful thing she had ever seen. Minutes later they had driven along the path the storm had taken; past uprooted trees and shattered houses. She hadn't understood why everyone spoke of it as a tragedy; to her it was a miracle. People spoke solemnly of the death and suffering the storm brought, but Mary suspected they were as pleased as she was. Death and suffering were familiar to them; drama was not.

Every time the sky darkened as it had done today, Mary hoped the miracle would return. She looked at her father, who had hardly seemed to notice the storm. He's dying in the same way the town is dying, she thought. Without dignity; without drama.

A dog began to bark nearby. The dog had noticed the storm, she was certain. It had been aware of nothing else; frightened, perhaps, but not absorbed in its own vague regrets. Maybe that's why we keep animals around us: to admire the simplicity of their reactions; to remind us of something we have lost. An innocence.

Seven

Despite what happened on the day of the storm, I still think of myself as a courageous animal. I now realize, though, that courage is a more complex matter than it once seemed to me. Not that I ever thought of it as simple.

In the beginning I imagined that to be courageous one had to be without fear. I chased automobiles; I pretended fearlessness. Then one day I saw one of my kind struck by an automobile. I watched the animal bleeding and twitching; I heard it whine. And I knew that some things should be feared. There was no point in challenging a machine. It was as futile as barking at thunder.

But some fears and threats had to be challenged or one could have no pride. Where was the line to be drawn? The answer became obvious when I was challenged to my first fight. I was frightened, but I didn't hesitate to accept the challenge. And after my victory I realized that one must never succumb to fear of another creature. It was honorable to flee from lightning, but not from an animal.

So as I stood on the porch during the storm, I felt no shame in wanting to follow the boy into the house to escape from the wind-driven rain and the hideous sound of the thunder. Yet I could not go into the house. Each time I moved towards the window I thought of the old woman, and I felt an emotion I had never known before. It resembled fear, but it must have been something else. One can fear a storm or another creature, but can one fear a quiet house or a memory? No. I was feeling something stronger than fear. And so I stayed on the porch, squinting against the wind and waiting for the next bolt of lightning to strike.

Does the boy understand why I wouldn't enter the house? I must be sure he realizes it had nothing to do with cowardice.

He must never doubt my courage.

2

Carl watched the small black mongrel walk along the edge of the pit. It moved nervously, staring at the piece of liver that lay below.

Not much of an opponent, the boy thought. But it was hard to be sure. The dogs that had come closest to testing Baxter had been small and seemingly timid.

What was it that made some fight and others not? Was it a matter of simple courage? Whatever the quality was, Carl suspected he didn't have it. He couldn't remember ever having been in a fight. He had seldom given anyone a reason to fight him. But there were always people who had been willing to fight *for* him. Not friends, necessarily, but those who were looking for someone to protect. Carl had sensed very early that some people were more willing to fight for others than for themselves. He made himself available to them. And now he was available to Baxter, who was next to him, straining against his leash.

The black dog dropped into the pit and picked up the liver. It looked up for a moment, as if seeking a way out, but then gave its attention to the meat. Carl released Baxter and watched him run to the pit, leap in, and take up his position. He had learned, after two dogs had escaped from the pit, to stand in front of the boxes that gave them a way out.

It was evident immediately that the black dog would not

fight. It dropped the meat and moved abjectly away from Baxter, wagging its tail. When Baxter moved towards it the dog lay down. It didn't respond even when Baxter charged and began nipping at its muzzle and ears. It wouldn't be provoked.

Baxter stood aside, leaving the escape path open. The other dog moved towards escape instantly, with an energy it had been carefully concealing. Baxter was ready for the move. He caught his victim's right hind leg in his jaws, forcing the dog quickly to its back. Then he stood aside and watched as it scrambled awkwardly up the boxes and limped away.

It was Baxter's sixth fight in the pit ... or the sixth time he had faced another dog there. Two of the encounters had involved some resistance; some contact. But no opponent had chosen to fight, and Baxter was unmarked except for a few small scratches inflicted by the nails of retreating paws. Few strong dogs were to be seen near the junk-yard now, and Carl had begun to look closely at the town's pets, judging their strength, looking for eyes that had the same expression as Baxter's.

Carl could not define the expression, and he saw it only occasionally; not in the eyes of pets, but in those of their owners.

3

It's the best moment of the evening, thought Sara Fine. But we won't remember it tomorrow. We'll remember that the beef was overdone; that there were silences while glances met briefly and shifted to rug or lap; that we drank too much.

She looked at Nancy and John Grafton. They were smiling expectantly at Jason, knowing that in a moment his silly, intricate story would end. They were his allies, hoping he would find the right final words; hoping to be delighted.

Even Carl seemed pleased. Sara had been surprised at how well he took her announcement of the dinner. No groans, no petulance. And now he was sitting willingly among them, clean and interested. He was staring at Nancy.

I've seen her body, Carl thought. He put his fingers into his back pocket and touched the key to the Prescott house. Each afternoon since the storm he had entered the empty house and stood in the front bedroom, staring across at the Graftons' second-floor windows, waiting for Nancy to appear for her nap. He knew how the sun glinted on the brass bed. He knew how she pulled her t-shirt over her head; how she stepped out of her jeans. He knew the outlines of her body, but not its details. He studied her now, learning the color of her eyes, the texture of her skin.

Nancy turned, laughing, to glance at Carl. He blushed and looked at his plate. He's still a child, she thought. Then she remembered Baxter, and her smile faded. Fortunately, the dog was avoiding them. They had heard it bark as they rang the doorbell, and they saw its squat white form retreat into the kitchen as they entered the house. It had not returned, but Nancy seldom forgot its presence.

John Grafton swallowed the last of his cognac. I've drunk too much, he thought. He looked around the dining-room, testing the focus of his eyes. He found himself looking at a photograph on the wall. It was an unframed enlargement, carefully exposed and printed, but it was strangely composed. John had no idea what its subject was. Something architectural, perhaps.

Sara noticed John's puzzled stare. She thought she had better say something in case he was about to make a critical remark. 'That's Carl's work,' she said.

John looked at the boy. It was a respectful look, Sara was relieved to see.

'I like it,' John said. He had always liked photographs. Whenever he went to a museum and saw a painting he had previously known from a photograph he invariably found he preferred the photograph to the original. He was disturbed by the largeness of paintings; by their texture and their traces of brush-strokes. Reproductions seemed more precise and less artificial to him. 'Was it taken here in town?' he asked.

'In the junk-yard,' Carl said.

'Do you have more of them?'

Carl's father answered for him: 'He does indeed. That was last summer's passion.'

John ignored Jason and continued to look at the boy. He sees things differently from the way we do, he thought. He wondered what Carl's passion was this summer. 'I'd like to see some of the others,' he said.

'They're pretty much all the same,' Carl said. Was the man really interested? No one else had ever been interested. The boy had spent hours in the basement darkroom the previous year. He hadn't used his camera often, but he was fascinated by the process of printing negatives. He remembered the excitement of standing in the yellow glow of the safe-light, watching the images slowly build up on the white paper.

He would print one negative again and again, changing the cropping or exposure slightly each time. One roll of film would last him for weeks. It was the manipulation of the images that absorbed him, not the images themselves. He had never photographed a person.

'Why don't you show Mr. Grafton some of the others, Carl?' his mother asked.

'Better yet,' John said, 'why don't you show us how you print them? I've never seen it done.'

'I don't do it any more. The chemicals aren't fresh. They wouldn't work.'

John looked at his wife. 'Wouldn't you like to see Carl print a picture?'

'Only if he wants to,' she said.

Carl thought of what it would be like to be in the dark-room with Mrs. Grafton. 'I guess I could try,' he said.

Minutes later he was in the basement with the Graftons. Were they just being polite? he wondered. Wouldn't they rather be upstairs with his parents? Maybe not. Maybe they were different.

The darkroom was a small, unventilated storage room. The acidic smell of his chemicals mingled with the scent of cognac and perfume. Carl filled the developing trays and put a negative in the enlarger. He talked softly, explaining the procedure. He exposed a sheet of paper and slid it into the developing fluid. He warned them not to expect too much; the fluid was old, and its temperature was not right. The three of them watched in silence as a vague grey shape began to appear on the submerged paper. Carl rocked the tray, and beneath the undulating liquid an image clarified: a small, featureless torso, staring eyes and twisted limbs. It was a broken, discarded doll.

Nancy shuddered, and John took her hand, both of them remembering the pool and the lifeless, submerged body of their child.

Carl was aware only of Nancy's body, which had been touching his as she looked over his shoulder.

Upstairs Jason Fine was helping Sara clear the dinner table.

'They seem to like Carl,' he said.

'It's easy to like other people's children,' Sara said. 'You can treat them as though they were adults. You don't have to try to understand them.'

'Have we tried to understand Carl?'

'Of course.'

'But we haven't been very successful at it.'

'No. Not at all, I suspect.'

But we understand each other, Jason thought. He felt the familiar but puzzling wave of affection growing in him. He took Sara into his arms. As they stood quietly holding each other it occurred to him that it had been years since he had embraced his son. It was an unthinkable act now.

'Do you ever embrace Carl?' he asked his wife.

'Oh, no.'

'Why not?'

'For the same reason you don't.'

'What's that?'

'He wouldn't allow it.'

'You don't think it's our fault then?'

'There's no fault involved. We embrace. Carl doesn't. It's not in his nature.'

Jason wondered what the boy's nature was . . . what he was becoming in these warm months of solitude. He opened his eyes and saw Baxter staring at him from the doorway to the kitchen.

'You're wrong,' he said to Sara. 'Carl does embrace. He embraces Baxter.'

4

At first Joseph Bartnik didn't understand the reason for his elation. He had left work and was driving home through the familiar streets of the town. It was a time of day when he usually felt little pleasure. Suddenly he understood. It was the first time since spring that the sun had not been visible above the elms as he approached Hawley Street. He looked at the leaves of the trees. They were losing their gloss. Soon, in a week perhaps, some leaves would begin to yellow, and the first one would drop to the ground.

Autumn pleased Mr. Bartnik. Not just because it was the hunting season, but because it ended the excesses of summer. He was tired of seeing things grow; he felt more comfortable when things around him were dying.

He sounded his horn as he passed the Cuzzo house. The old man and his daughter waved from the porch. Mary was wearing shorts and a halter. She would be back at the school soon, her body covered as it should be at her age. She would prevent the children of the town from doing what they wanted to do. Mr. Bartnik respected teachers.

Queenie was waiting for him at the door. He lifted her into his arms. She's gaining weight, he thought. Under his supporting hand her belly was thick, but not flabby. And there was swelling at her nipples.

'God,' he said, and dropped the dog. He would rather have his daughter pregnant than his spaniel.

He walked slowly towards the back of the house. When he reached his gun rack he touched the stock of his favorite deer rifle. He could see Veronica in the kitchen. She was standing at the stove, staring into a frying pan and watching grease accumulate around half-cooked hamburgers. He wished she were a deer standing in a clearing.

He dropped his hand and went upstairs to his bedroom. There were tears in his eyes.

5

Someone was in the bunker. Carl could see candlelight behind the partially closed door. What should he do? As the boy tried to decide Baxter trotted to the bunker's entrance and barked. The doorway opened fully, and Veronica Bartnik appeared.

'Hello, Baxter,' she said. 'You're going to be a father.'

The dog backed away.

'Veronica?' Carl said. He was surprised at how young she looked.

'Did you hear my news?'

'About Baxter?'

'Yes. My father's really pissed off.'

Carl didn't like to hear girls talk that way.

Veronica walked towards him, brushing off her jeans. Her breasts shook beneath her t-shirt. The boy wondered why he was able to watch her with such calmness.

'What are you doing here?' he asked.

'I don't think I should go home tonight. I thought I might stay here. Would you mind?'

Yes, I would, Carl thought. He was spending little time in the bunker now that he had the key to the Prescott house. But the hideaway was still important to him; it belonged to him. He only borrowed the house.

'I know a better place,' he said.

Veronica was impressed with the change that had taken place in Carl. A few weeks ago he would have been delighted to find her in the bunker. He would have begged her to lie there with him. She sensed that he still wanted her, but only on his own terms. It was the kind of relationship that interested her the most; a relationship she had previously formed only with much older boys. She took Carl's hand and said, 'I think I'd rather stay here.'

'You can't,' he said.

I'm right, she thought. I no longer control him. 'Where is the other place?'

'I'll show you,' Carl said. 'Just a minute.' He went into the bunker. The contents of his picture box were scattered on the rug. He replaced them, blew out the candle, and put the door back in place. He returned to Veronica and took her hand. He led her back to the town, through quiet alleys, to the back door of the Prescott house.

Baxter stopped at the foot of the steps and watched the boy and girl enter the house.

Carl had hardly been aware of Veronica as they walked

through the town, but when the door closed behind them he became vividly conscious of her. He wasn't sure whether he enjoyed the sensation. He released her hand.

'Carl,' she said. 'Stay with me. I can't see anything.'

Carl moved away from her.

'This is the old woman's house, isn't it?' the girl said. 'The one who died.'

Carl didn't answer.

'Carl, are you trying to scare me? That's what little boys do.'

'You can leave if you want to.'

He *is* still a boy, she thought. But he was not the boy who sat silently across the aisle from her last spring. He had learned something since then. She wanted to find out what.

Carl waited for her. He heard her moving cautiously toward him. Her groping hand touched his arm. Her fingers rested lightly against his sleeve for a few seconds and then moved inside his shirt and across his hairless chest, coming to rest on a tiny contracted nipple.

Carl shuddered. A month ago he would have been grateful for the gesture; he would have welcomed her instruction. But he was no longer in awe of sex. Not since the night he watched Baxter and Queenie. Lately, lying in the bunker or on Mrs. Prescott's bed, he had begun to realize that experience wasn't necessarily more important than imagination. Veronica had learned her gestures from books or from the older boys at school. Carl had seen the books . . . cynically written and carelessly printed; and he had talked to the boys . . . smug and unimaginative.

Veronica was experienced, but so was Baxter. Carl didn't envy either of them their experience. He had something more important; something neither of them could understand.

The girl moved closer to him. He remembered the closeness of Nancy Grafton in the darkroom. Did Mrs. Grafton understand him? She could learn to, he thought.

'Hold me,' Veronica said. 'You're not afraid, are you?'

'No. You're afraid.'

He's right, she thought. She wanted to think of the darkness as romantic; to find Carl's reticence exciting. But she was uneasy.

Carl took her hand and began to lead her out of the kitchen. 'I'll show you where you can sleep,' he said.

They went haltingly up the stairs. When they reached the landing Carl stopped. Since discovering the house he had asked people about Mrs. Prescott's death. He knew all the details now, including one no one else seemed to know.

'This is where they found her,' he whispered.

'I don't want to know about that,' Veronica said. I should leave, she thought. She moved to go back down the stairs, but Carl pulled her back and they started up the second flight.

When they reached the bedroom Veronica began to relax. Through the windows she could see lights in the neighboring houses. She became aware of the arousal that underlay her fear. Carl had gone to a window and was looking across the street. She kicked her shoes off and went to stand behind him, letting her breasts touch his back. She reached quickly around Carl's body and let her hand rest on his crotch. It was as soft as a child's.

Carl pulled her hand away and turned to face her. She was embarrassed for him. How much easier it would be, she thought, if men could pretend sexual excitement. A woman can deceive . . . not only the man, but herself. A man's failure was undeniable. She began to feel a fondness for the boy. It might have been based on pity, but the emotion was genuine. She wanted him to succeed.

'What is it you want me to do?' she asked. 'I'll do it, but you have to tell me what it is. Tell me the words for it. The short words.'

'I want you to shut up,' Carl said. His humiliation was sudden and profound. He needed revenge. Baxter knew about revenge.

He went to the dresser and searched in a drawer until he found one of Mrs. Prescott's nightgowns. He handed it to Veronica. 'Put this on,' he said. 'And then we'll play a game.'

Veronica hesitated. Carl's face seemed impassive in the dim light. She needed a clue to his mood. Was there tension at the corners of his mouth; a suppressed smile? Were his eyes narrowed slightly in anger? Words are important in the darkness, she thought, and she hadn't understood Carl's words. She waited for him to speak again, but the silence was broken only by laughter from a neighbor's television set; the laughter of an audience. Like the bleating of distant sheep.

A game. What kind of game? She raised her hand reluctantly and took the nightgown. It smelled old and stale. She walked to the bed, dropped the gown on it, and turned to face Carl, her hands on the zipper of her jeans.

He was leaving the room. 'We need Baxter,' he said.

Carl moved quickly along the corridor. When he reached the head of the stairs he paused. They'll stand here, he thought; the girl and Baxter. I won't have to explain the game to Baxter.

He started down the stairs, wondering why he had not wanted to see Veronica's body; why he was not aroused. Later, maybe. He opened the back door and whispered Baxter's name. He looked for the pale figure among the shadows, but saw nothing. He walked through the yard and into the alley. The dog had gone. There could be no game now.

Carl started slowly back to the house. Baxter had failed him for the first time. The boy was offended and puzzled. Had the dog left because of boredom or because of fear?

As Carl re-entered the bedroom he heard the back door

slam. It was probably Veronica running away. He was relieved. He forgot the girl immediately and lay down on the bed, the nightgown wrinkling beneath him. He thought of Baxter. And it occurred to him for the first time that the dog might not return. He's free, Carl thought. He can walk away: shit on the street and walk away; get Queenie pregnant and walk away; kill and walk away. Why shouldn't animals be held responsible for their actions?

Before Carl left the house to look for Baxter he realized that the emotion he was feeling was not anger but envy.

Eight

As I waited for the boy I became aware of the change in the night air. It contained the aroma of decay, and although the breeze that ruffled my fur was not cold, it was subtly penetrating. The season was changing. Did the boy notice? I doubted it. He would notice only when it became necessary for him to put on more and heavier clothing; when the leaves began to fall.

Humans are not observant. I know, because I sometimes become careless and adopt their habits. I concern myself with shadows; with the old woman, for example, who no longer exists. But the night air exists, and it is a mistake to forget it. The boy forgets. The girl and the shadows of the old woman's house absorb him; they restrict his freedom.

It is obvious that people are not interested in freedom. They restrict themselves in too many ways. It surprises me that they do not put leashes on one another as they do on us. The older people in particular seem obsessed with restraint. It is evident even in the way they move about; never running, but walking slowly, always on the same side of the walk. They pause at corners and cross the streets together, proceeding past their neat rows of buildings. They ignore the people who pass them, stepping aside when necessary, never snarling or sniffing at anyone. Sometimes they pause to look into one another's eyes and chatter, never showing the anger or attraction I sometimes sense in them.

The children are different. They move about freely, and I

have even seen one of them urinate on the street. But they are controlled by the older people, and eventually they all seem to lose their sense of freedom. I suppose even the boy might eventually become as passive and uninteresting as his parents. But it is difficult to judge the boy. He seeks his freedom in subtle ways, and I must be ready for many possibilities. He knows of my courage, but he must also know that I live by my own rules, and that I will tolerate him only as long as he does not oppose those rules.

I realized that on the night he was in the house with the girl. I walked away from him to remind him of my independence. I didn't go far; just to his parents' house. I waited for him at the front door, knowing that unlike me he must always return to that door.

2

Jason Fine switched off the record player and said to his wife, 'Carl's later than usual, isn't he?'

'Yes. I suppose we should talk to him about it.'

'Do you know where he goes?'

'Just out, he says. With the other kids.'

Jason tried to remember what he had done on summer nights when he was Carl's age. It seemed to him he had spent most of his time trailing behind older boys, watching them and admiring their audacity and ingenuity. But had they really been older than he? Maybe not. Maybe they had just been more . . . more what? Not more intelligent. No one got better grades than he did. But he had never been a leader away from the classroom.

He admired the boys that had the courage to cut classes and who seemed to have no fears; those who would steal candy bars from the drugstore; those who played football in the vacant lot and would get up smiling after being thrown to the grassless, stony ground. Jason didn't play those games, but he watched them carefully. He preferred watching them to sitting quietly, playing and winning a chess game.

Sara walked to the window and looked out into the night. Carl likes the darkness just as I do, she thought. And he likes to wander through the town as Jason does. Why do we always blame our children for having our own traits? Then she noticed the pallid form lying in the shadows of the porch.

She turned to her husband. 'I think Baxter's out there.'

Jason went to the door and called the dog's name.

Baxter got up and started towards the door. But then he stopped and looked out into the darkness. Carl was coming up the walk.

'He's here,' the boy said. 'I've been looking all over town for him. How long has he been here?'

'I don't know,' Sara said. 'We've just discovered him.'

Baxter was standing between Sara and Jason. He was staring at Carl, but there was no sign that he even recognized the boy.

'What happened?' Jason asked.

'He just ran away from me,' Carl said.

Sara looked down at the dog. 'Maybe he's sick.' She knelt down next to him, steadying him with one hand and touching his nose with the other. She had seldom been this close to the dog. She felt his thick muscles move as he turned his head. He's stronger than any of us, she thought. She was glad he wasn't her enemy.

Jason squatted and ran his hand over Baxter's body, pressing and probing. The dog stood passively while the man examined him. 'He doesn't seem to be hurt,' Jason said. 'But he's tense. Maybe something frightened him.'

'Maybe,' Carl said. He was disturbed to see his parents giving so much attention to Baxter. Was the dog becoming fond of them?

Carl started towards Baxter, who backed away and trotted into the house.

'Sorry I was late,' Carl said, and followed the dog upstairs.

Sara watched them disappear into the boy's bedroom. 'A lover's quarrel,' she said.

'Something like that, I suppose,' Jason answered. 'Do you think he loves the dog?'

'They seem to have a lot in common.'

'Is that good?'

'It's better than nothing.'

Jason felt an unpleasant emotion that might have been either guilt or jealousy. He didn't like to be reminded that Carl might be capable of affection; that the distance between them might not be the boy's fault.

'What has Baxter got that we haven't?' he asked Sara.

'Beastliness?'

Carl sat on the edge of his bed, and Baxter lay in the corner of the room. They both watched the chain that dangled from the boy's hand. It was the chain he had used in training Baxter: a noose of sharp-studded metal that looped around the dog's neck, tightening and biting into muscle when it was pulled. He hasn't forgotten it, Carl thought. He'll never forget it. But I've been careless in not reminding him.

The boy walked across the room and put the chain on the dresser, next to several notebooks he had used in school the previous year. He opened one of the books and leafed through pages covered with his precise handwriting; words and numbers that reminded him of nothing but tedious hours in the classroom. Those hours would begin again soon, and there would be less time to spend with Baxter. Their bond must be strengthened before then. How?

Carl turned out the light and lay on the bed. He heard the faint but urgent sound of his father talking to his mother in their bedroom; he heard the noises of the town diminish. Sounds were more important to him than they had been previously. He wondered whether he could trade his camera for a tape recorder. It would be easier to record the town aurally than visually. People are too aware of the way they look; they disguise themselves.

Miss Cuzzo, for example: she dresses and moves carefully, and her appearance as she stands before the class inspires respect. But there is a weakness in her voice. Even the slight squeak of her breathing reveals her discomfort as she walks through the quiet aisles, watching her students write in their notebooks. Carl wanted to record those sounds and play them back at night as he would have looked at a photograph taken through her bathroom window.

He listened for the sound of Baxter's breathing, but could not isolate it from the noise of crickets and wind-rustled leaves. Baxter: what was to be done about him? The dog must do something for me, Carl thought. Something unforgettable. Something unmentionable.

3

Jimmy Benson liked people and money. Because of that, and because he was ten years old, he was widely admired in the town. Tired home-owners liked to see him struggling eagerly but inefficiently behind a lawn-mower; they liked the moment when they pressed money into his small hand and watched his undisguised joy at being overtipped.

Jimmy often did chores for Mary Cuzzo and her father. For a time Mary thought the boy might be one of the rare children without a major flaw in his personality, and then one day she asked him to clean out a storage room in her basement. As she explained the job to him she saw his admiration for the cluttered room. He didn't understand the need to discard; to bring order. And she realized he never spent the money he earned. He would not become a likable man.

There were few places in town that Jimmy found more attractive than the junk-yard, but he avoided it when Carl and Baxter were there. Even if Carl had welcomed him, he would have stayed away. He didn't understand Carl's interest in the yard; he knew only that it was not the same as his own.

The younger boy often went to the junk-yard when the sun was rising. He dug and sorted in the dew-wet trash, retrieving objects that could be sold. He dragged a plastic bag behind him, hearing the clink of scrap metal against soft-drink bottles, wondering at the extravagance of the people of the town. When a bag was filled he stored it temporarily in the strange circular pit that someone had constructed.

He was starting to climb out of the pit one morning when he looked up to see Carl Fine standing above him. The sun was behind Carl, and Jimmy's eyes began to water as he squinted up, trying to smile at the older boy.

'Hi, Carl. I'm getting some bottles.'

Carl didn't answer.

Jimmy continued, 'I've got about a dollar's worth. I guess. That's about enough for one day.' He lifted the bag and started to climb out of the pit, but Carl blocked his way. He was standing above the only part of the wall that could be scaled easily. Then Jimmy saw Baxter, who was standing behind Carl, at the end of a long leash. A metal collar glittered around the dog's neck.

'Why don't you stay there for a minute?' Carl said. 'I've got a surprise for you.'

Jimmy moved back towards the center of the pit.

Carl leaned over and removed the collar from Baxter. 'Now you can do something for me,' he whispered. Then he picked the dog up and dropped him into the pit.

Jimmy backed farther away, watching Baxter carefully. Glass shattered as the boy dropped his bag. Then there was silence as Baxter took his position in front of the pit's escape route.

The trapped boy had no doubt about the danger of the situation. He knew Carl's mind. They had sometimes played together in the junk-yard the previous summer. The game was what Carl called 'World War II'. The setting was always the ruins of Berlin, and the actions never varied. 'You be an American G.I.,' Carl would say. 'I'll be a German officer. The Russians are at the edge of the city.' Jimmy would listen in vague embarrassment as Carl explained intensely that the Russians were the true enemy, and that the Allies and the Third Reich must unite against them. Then the boys would fight the imaginary enemy.

Jimmy had not forgotten Carl's abandonment in those battles: the saliva that gathered at the corners of his mouth as he writhed on the ground in supposed hand-to-hand combat; the tears that sometimes appeared in his eyes at the end of the game as they stood to be decorated by a grateful Führer.

And now, as he stood in the pit, Jimmy understood that he had become the enemy. It was not a time for reasoning or jokes. His safety depended on the reactions of the dog. Without the dog there could have been no danger. Carl didn't fight real people . . . not even small, weak ones.

The dog was another matter, Jimmy thought, as he looked into Baxter's small, unpleasant eyes. The dog would fight, but would he fight with no reason except to satisfy Carl's vicious whims? Jimmy could only put himself at the dog's mercy. He sat down very slowly. Then he rolled over on his side, drawing his knees up to his chest and wrapping his arms around them. He lowered his head and tried to suppress his fear, but as the cool dampness of the earth penetrated his clothing he began to tremble. He closed his eyes tightly.

'Baxter. Get him, Baxter.' It was Carl's voice. Jimmy

waited for the attack, but it didn't come. In the distance he heard an electric lawn-mower start up, and he longed to be in town, smelling the newly cut grass; smiling at the harmless, generous grown-ups.

Then there was a faint scrabbling sound near him, and he heard Carl call the dog's name again. But this time there was a strained quality in the voice: desperation or even fear.

'Come back, Baxter.'

Jimmy opened his eyes. The dog was no longer in the pit with him. Carl still stood above, but his back was turned. The younger boy stood up, his legs trembling. He could see the dog sitting near by on high ground. I'm safe, Jimmy thought. He watched as Carl walked towards Baxter. The dog snarled.

Jimmy climbed carefully out of the pit. There was no need to hurry; they had forgotten him. He walked slowly away, feeling neither anger nor fear, for he understood now that he had never really been in danger. Either Carl or Baxter was in danger. Or maybe they both were.

4

The boy has misjudged me. He doesn't understand that although I have killed, I have not done so without having reasons . . . my own reasons. I have killed when my situation was intolerable or when I was being threatened. I would not kill for another, particularly not for the boy, whose reasons are so foreign to me. Until I was forced into the pit with the younger boy it had not occurred to me that any creature could be interested in killing for its own sake. But I am sure now that the boy has such an interest.

After I realized what he wanted me to do, I didn't know whether to fear him or admire him. And for a few moments I wouldn't allow him to touch me. But I knew he was harmless, and that in his clumsy way he was paying tribute to my strength and courage. The boy was no threat to me, and now he would understand my nature more clearly than ever. We would continue as before.

But there are times when I am near sleep that I recall the obvious eagerness and pleasure the boy felt when he made me face the other boy. I must never forget the treachery of that act.

PART THREE

One

It was the first day of the fall term. Mary Cuzzo's class sat uncomfortably before her, filling in registration forms.

I'm a doctor, she thought. Her students looked to her as if they had been exposed to a disease. They seemed feverish, their sun-reddened faces frowning over the intricacy of the act she had asked them to perform. Pens were held with the awkwardness reserved for unwanted, unfamiliar objects. Eyes that had become accustomed to open sky were puzzled by the delicate shapes of printed words. The delirium of the young minds was real; there was a sense of mortality in the quiet room. Bright, dead leaves drifted past the windows.

It was Miss Cuzzo's favorite time of year. Even if she hadn't been a teacher, she would have thought of the fall as being the most significant season. A season for death, she thought. Even the children understand that.

She thought of her father and the summer she had spent with him in the dark house. The old man conserved his life beyond the point of dignity. His daughter's presence obviously irritated him. She thought at first that he was envious of her energy, and she began to cultivate lethargy. It was a role she enjoyed. I offer you my languor, she thought, as she lay silently on her bed in the afternoon.

But her father was not interested in her vitality or her lack of it; he was occupied only with conserving his own energy, which he gave up grudgingly. He seldom spoke, and in recent weeks he had, in his concern with conservation, even begun to take a secret pleasure in his frequent periods of constipation. He was happy when classes resumed and he no longer had to give her even the slight attention she required.

Veronica Bartnik concentrated on filling in the forms that lay on her desk. She wrote the information carefully: name, address, age. Why did the simple facts seem so odd; as if they described a stranger? Perhaps because she changed and the facts did not.

She was conscious of the many things that had changed since last spring: Carl, for example. She had hardly been aware of him then. But today, when she entered the classroom, he dominated her thoughts. It had been difficult for her to decide whether to sit behind him or in front of him; whether to see him or be seen by him. She didn't want either. She didn't want to be in the same room with him.

It's better not to know too much about people, she thought. Why had she listened to Carl's talk about Hitler? She would never forget that. Why hadn't they just silently coupled the way the dogs had? The dogs had already forgotten ... even Queenie, who would be having her litter any day.

Veronica envied dogs. Maybe she always had. She remembered that when she first heard the phrase 'a dog's life' she had assumed it referred to a life of ease and comfort; a good life. It still seemed that way to her. Dogs don't get to know anyone too well; they have no regrets. She sometimes wondered whether she was becoming more dog-like. She had become less interested in her appearance. A year ago she would not have worn the loose, bulky, breast-concealing sweater she was wearing today.

Could a person become a dog? The way you could become a werewolf? Why not?

She's behind me, Carl thought. I can almost smell her.

He hadn't talked to Veronica since the night in Mrs. Prescott's house. He had seen her occasionally on the streets of the town; had watched her turn nervously away from him. It was the first time anyone had ever been afraid of him. He was pleased.

The boy looked up from his desk to see Miss Cuzzo's eyes turn away from his. She's too clean, he thought. During the summer when he had passed her house on quiet afternoons and evenings he had heard the sound of running water from her second-floor bathroom; sometimes two and three times on the same day.

Carl no longer enjoyed bathing. When he was younger it had pleased him to stand in the shower, soaping and resoaping his body; breathing the steam-moistened air. He would imagine particles of dirt mingling with the draining water. But now the water seemed to threaten him. The smell of soap offended him. There were nights when he ran the shower only so that his parents would hear it. Instead of entering the shower stall he would stand outside before the mirror, examining the pale hairs that had appeared in his armpits; aware of the new odor about him. He was proud of the odor. He didn't want to lose it.

When the class was dismissed Carl turned and smiled at Veronica. She pretended not to see him and hurried from the room. Carl caught up with her in the corridor. She heard his voice behind her.

'Hello, Eva.'

She didn't answer. She was disconcerted to find that she enjoyed hearing the secret name. Secrecy had always appealed to her. Maybe Carl knew that; maybe it was a weakness he recognized in her and took advantage of.

He was beside her now. 'I just wanted you to know I'm sorry about that night in the old lady's house,' he said. 'I didn't mean to scare you. It was just a game.'

A secret game, Veronica thought. He knows more about those things than I do. He's reminding me that shared secrets create a bond.

She still didn't respond, but she stopped. They were standing in one of the patches of sunlight that fell from the overhead windows.

'How's Queenie?' Carl asked.

'All right. She'll have her puppies soon.'

Veronica looked at the boy. The harsh backlight silhouetted his head, illuminating the thickening down on his jaws and chin. It's like puppy fur, she thought. It's time for him to start shaving. One of the rules she used to have was that she would ignore boys who weren't old enough to shave every day. She shouldn't have broken the rule. 'I have to go,' she said.

'That's okay. You don't have to be friendly with me,' Carl said. 'But maybe I can do you a favor some time. I owe you a favor.'

He smiled and walked away.

Veronica frowned. She disliked his pleasant manner. Maybe that's what she had learned from him: to mistrust charm . . . even her own. She watched him walk out of the sunlight and into the shadows. And she wondered about the secrets he hadn't shared with her.

2

The woman is not without her virtues. Now that the boy is away so often, I have begun to observe her more carefully. We share the house together through most of the day, never touching; glancing at each other occasionally. She often sits for hours looking at the peculiar little black marks on the pages of her books. She smiles, and I can see her toes curl in her open-fronted slippers. Sometimes, when she puts her book aside and goes into the kitchen or bathroom, I jump on to her chair and lie on the soft cushion while it is still warm from her body and rich with her scent. She does not excite me or interest me in the way the boy does, and she makes no effort to understand me, but I find it comforting to be with her. I would not harm her.

I think she understands the importance of repose. Except when she makes the sounds on her instrument, she does not waste her energy the way most humans do. She does not walk aimlessly about the town or engage in the more meaningless activities the others occupy themselves with. She does not gather and burn the fallen leaves.

We sit together, aware of each other, but feeling neither like nor dislike. She has taught me the value of indifference. It is something the boy has yet to learn. When he returns to the house in the afternoon he brings with him not only energy but passionate attitudes. The woman can remain indifferent even to him, but I immediately share his excitement. I remember the feelings I had towards the old woman, the couple and the child. And I consider the feelings I now have for the boy.

He no longer lets me run freely beside him. He keeps the chain tightened against my throat; guiding me; making sounds of command. I would not tolerate such treatment if I did not sense the respect in his voice. And I wonder if the day will come when the respect will no longer be there. I wonder whether he could ever be so foolish.

3

Joseph Bartnik stood shivering in his sleep-wrinkled underwear. He stared down into the cardboard box, where the four pink-and-white puppies nuzzled against Queenie's belly.

They're disgusting, he thought. They could be anything:

pigs, rats, even some kind of human abortion. He squatted and looked at the featureless, wrinkled faces; the stunted legs. I should do it now, he thought, while their eyes are closed. He imagined one of the tiny skulls between his thumb and forefinger, yielding to his grip like a hard-boiled egg. He reached into the box.

Queenie snarled.

The man withdrew his hand and stood up. It was the first time the dog had ever threatened him. It's too late, he thought. She's no longer mine. She'll stay in the house, nursing, protecting, not remembering the quiet ponds, the ducks against the dawn sky.

'Have they been born?' It was Veronica. 'Are they all right?' She came to stand next to her father. She wondered whether she was too late. For the past few nights she had slept fitfully, rising often and walking through the dark house to look in the corner of the kitchen where the dog slept. She hadn't wanted her father to be the first to find the puppies. She imagined him tightening the top of a plastic bag.

The animals were safe, though; and white, as she knew they would be.

'They have to go,' her father said.

'No.'

'They're ugly and useless.'

'Why don't you put some clothes on?'

Mr. Bartnik hesitated and then started out of the room. 'They have to go,' he said.

The girl knelt beside the box and looked down at the four pale forms. She was not pleased. They *are* ugly and useless, she thought. She had never seen newborn creatures before. They weren't the attractive, playful animals she had expected. They were alien to the light and air, like grotesque, beached fish; accustomed to silence and darkness. But aren't we all like that at birth? We learn to forget the darkness. Most of us do.

Veronica's father was back in the kitchen. He took the dented percolator from the stove and filled it, measuring water and coffee precisely. 'It was that boy's dog, wasn't it? The one at the junk-yard.'

'Yes.' There was no point in denying it.

'He's the worst kind of dog there is. He's worse than useless. He's a fighter.'

'How do you know that?'

'I know about dogs. He shouldn't be allowed to reproduce.'

'You can't decide that. You're not God.'

'I'm a man.'

The worst kind there is, Veronica thought. She knew she didn't dare leave the puppies with him. 'Will you make a deal with me?' she asked. 'If you wait until the puppies can leave Queenie I'll get rid of them for you. Just a few weeks. She can still go hunting with you.'

'They might ruin her for hunting. They might have done it already.'

'And she might never forgive you if you take them away from her now.'

Mr. Bartnik looked at the dogs and then at his daughter. 'We can keep them for four weeks,' he said. 'That's all. Duck season opens in five weeks. That gives her a week to forget them.'

Can I trust him? Veronica wondered. The next few days would be crucial. After that the pups would begin to look like dogs. Not even her father could kill them then. He was jealous and unpleasant, but he was not a monster.

'You promise you won't harm them?'

'I'll give you four weeks,' her father said. He was looking at Queenie.

He loves the dog, Veronica thought. And he loves my mother. Thank God he doesn't love me.

4

'Do they have blue eyes?' Carl asked.

'I don't know. Their eyes aren't open yet.'

'But they look like Baxter?'

'They will, I think. They're white.'

Why is she telling me this? Carl wondered. And why am I so excited by it?

'Could I see them?' he asked. He saw the girl hesitate. 'I don't mean could I come to your house. Maybe you could bring them out some time ... some time when I'm with Baxter. He ought to see them.'

'They're too young for that now. But maybe when they're older ... before I give them away.'

We'll meet in the bunker, Carl thought. But he wouldn't suggest it. He would smile and be patient. She would make the suggestion, just as she had announced the birth.

She would come to the bunker some night, making her way carefully through the rubbish, carrying a cardboard box. She would return the young animals to the place where they were conceived; to the one responsible for their conception. Baxter would be pleased.

Two

They have my scent. It is a weak scent, and impure, but there can be no doubt. They are feeble and unobservant. They have the failings that all young creatures seem to have. They are innocent.

The boy and girl lift the creatures one by one from the box, placing them on the rug of the hideaway. In the dim candlelight we watch their ridiculous attempts to walk. I am not amused, as the boy and girl seem to be. I watch them stroke the tiny white bodies, and I listen as they mumble quietly to each other, to me, and to the young ones.

Humans seem to be fascinated by any kind of infancy. I see them stop in the streets of the town to lean over baby carriages. The women in particular gaze at the infants with obvious devotion, as though they see a great virtue in helplessness. I suppose it is easy to love a creature that is totally dependent on you and to imagine that it loves you in return. But I do not see the point of such emotions.

I wonder whether I would try to protect even these four pitiful animals. Perhaps. But would I be protecting them or my own scent, which they somehow share?

2

Veronica was aroused and frightened. There were too many of them in the bunker: Carl, Baxter, the puppies. The shelter was too cold and too dark. Even the puppies looked sinister in the deep shadows. And yet she knew she would remember this night as she often remembered the night in the Prescott house: she would recall it as she lay with other boys, and she would find the memory of Carl's dangerous immaturity more exciting than the presence and conventional passion of the others.

I must talk, she thought. 'Do you think Baxter knows they're his?'

'He knows. But he doesn't care.'

'How do you know what he thinks?'

'I understand him.'

The girl looked at Carl and then at Baxter. They do understand each other, she thought. Too well.

Carl began to put the puppies back in their box. 'I suppose you'd better take them back,' he said. 'They might catch cold or something.'

'I can't take them back.'

'Why not?'

'My father doesn't want them to be with Queenie any more.'

'What are you going to do with them?'

'I was going to give them away, but nobody wants them.'

'Why not?'

'I'm not sure.' She was sure now, but she could not admit it to Carl. Baxter was not admired in the town. People were interested in her offer until they found out that the puppies were his; that they looked like him.

'Then what happens to them?'

'You said you'd do me a favor, Carl. Take the dogs.'

'All of them?'

'They're yours in a way.'

The boy looked at the puppies. He picked one up and began to pet it. 'I guess they are,' he said. 'Sure, I'll take them. Why not?'

Veronica leaned over and kissed him. 'Thank you,' she said. He hardly seemed to notice her.

It was not until Veronica lay in her bed that night that she recalled the story Carl had told her about Hitler's dog and the killing of its puppies during the last days in the Berlin bunker. And she knew she had made an unforgivable mistake.

She did not sleep that night. She listened to Queenie, who wandered through the house, whimpering and searching.

3

After the girl had gone Carl chained Baxter outside the bunker and lay down alone inside with the puppies. There's so little life in them, he thought; such undefined life. They're like weeds that could be stepped on unnoticed in the darkness. I could walk away, just as Baxter walked away from the old woman, from the child, and from the stray mongrel that challenged him.

Four lives. Powerless and unthreatening creatures, but with the form of Baxter, whose power and courage the boy coveted. Four lives that had and could have no meaning. But four deaths could have a meaning.

Carl picked up one of the puppies, enclosing its body in his left hand, feeling the faint, rapid heartbeat within its warm softness. He took its head in his right hand. 'Old lady Prescott,' he said, and he twisted his hands, slowly and relentlessly, until there was a snap; until he no longer felt the heartbeat.

Then the second puppy. 'The Grafton baby.'

The third. 'The mongrel.'

He picked up the last puppy in wet, trembling hands. 'And one more, Baxter. One more.'

Carl blew out the candle and lay back, suddenly aware of the coldness of the air. He felt an emotion that had become familiar to him in recent months: the sudden depression that followed masturbation. The moment of incredible contrast, when the ecstasy vanished and he was left with the mess and the guilt.

But that feeling would pass. Clean up the mess, recall the pleasure. He groped for the box and dragged it to the exit. Moving quickly out of Baxter's sight, he carried the box a few yards away and covered it with trash. He felt the delicate graininess of frost on the objects he was moving. His hands felt cleansed. Things were better now.

He returned to Baxter. As he led the dog towards the town he felt a strength he had not felt before. It was the first time he had not known a vague fear of the power that was transmitted to his hand through the leash. He pulled hard, tightening the chain around the dog's neck.

'Heel, Baxter. Heel.'

4

Nancy Grafton paused on her front steps. Carl and Baxter were coming towards her. She wouldn't have recognized the boy in the darkness, but the dog was unmistakable. Should she wait and say hello? She hadn't spoken to the boy since the night of the dinner. She remembered his politeness and his occasional interested glances. He was fond of her. She waited.

As the boy and the dog neared her Baxter began to pull away towards the street. She no longer feared the dog, but it still repelled her. It was panting heavily, its condensing breath obscuring its features.

'Hello, Mrs. Grafton.'

'Hello, Carl.' The boy seemed agitated; elated. Nancy wondered whether he had been with a girl.

The front door opened behind her. It was John. 'It's too cold to be gossiping on the street,' he said. 'Why doesn't everyone come in?'

No, Nancy thought, not the dog.

'Maybe for a minute,' Carl said. 'But I'll tie Baxter out here. He might track up your floor.'

Nancy was surprised at the boy's self-assurance. A few weeks ago he wouldn't have accepted the invitation; he wouldn't have realized that Baxter wasn't wanted. The boy looked stronger and less attractive than she had remembered. But he still looked at her with interest. She preferred an admiring person to an attractive one.

The house was warm. Nancy sat quietly as John talked to Carl, who looked intently around the room. Did the boy admire the house? She doubted it. Young people aren't interested in formal shelter. But something intrigued him.

'You haven't seen the house before, have you, Carl?' Nancy asked.

The boy started to reply, but shook his head instead.

'We'll give you a tour,' John said. 'It's one of the more boring rituals adults inflict on one another. We'll initiate you.'

As they walked through the house Nancy became aware of a sureness in Carl's movements; a lack of surprise. It's as if he knew what to expect, she thought.

They were at the door to the couple's bedroom. Nancy started past it, but Carl paused.

'It's messy, I'm afraid,' she said. She walked into the room and picked up a nightgown from the floor. Carl followed her. He went slowly to the brass bed and put his hand on it.

Nancy watched uncomfortably as he stared at the rumpled bedspread and the pushed-aside woolen throw. What is he thinking? she wondered. She remembered having the same thought about Baxter when the dog first came to live with them. Then it occurred to her that Carl and Baxter were alike in many ways: silent, observant, attentive. And dangerous, perhaps?

John apparently didn't think so. He led the way back to the parlor, and talked enthusiastically to Carl about the attractions of junk-yards. They're like brothers, Nancy thought. Her husband would make a better brother than a father. There was too much responsibility in fatherhood; too many occasions to be unlikable. He would want Carl to visit them again.

As the boy left John said, 'Stop by again some time. Or maybe you can show me around the junk-yard.'

Carl looked pleased. As Nancy shook hands with him she noticed how strong his grip was. There were short white hairs on the front of his jacket. The hairs of a small animal.

Three

The boy must die.

This morning, after he left the house, and the woman let me into the yard, I could think only of the four helpless animals the boy had shown me in the hideaway. I knew they could not survive long on their own. And even though I realized no creature is another's responsibility, I could not forget that they had my scent; they were my kind. I went to them.

It was good to be free in the town. There was no chain at my neck, and the boy was not nearby making his sounds of command. As I moved through the streets people moved aside, sensing my determination; knowing that without the boy I was more to be respected than ever. I moved quickly along the familiar route, not allowing myself to be distracted by odors or sounds.

But despite my eagerness to get to the edge of town, it was difficult for me not to stop. It occurred to me how fond I had become of the streets; how well I knew them. Was I beginning to understand the way the people felt about the town? They didn't own the town; they shared it. Maybe the important thing was that the town gave them something to be mutually familiar with. The old woman had known the streets as I now knew them; as the four small white creatures would know them.

I located the animals immediately, although it took me some time to uncover their limp, twisted bodies. There could be no doubt about what had been done or who had done it. Mingled with the scent of death was that of the boy.

I knew at once that he must die. He had crossed the line between the willing of death and the causing of it. He had challenged me.

And so I wait among the discarded objects, which glitter with the moisture of sun-melted frost. When the sun is lower in the sky the boy will come for me. He will find me in the center of the circle he built; the circle in which he has so often urged me to kill. I will need no urging today.

2

'Where's Baxter?' Carl asked his mother.

'Isn't he in the yard?'

'No. He's gone.'

'He'll be back.'

She doesn't care about the dog, Carl thought. She doesn't care about me. 'You left the gate open.'

'I didn't leave it open. I left it unlocked. It's always un-locked.'

'He could get hurt. He could get hit by a car.'

'Baxter can take care of himself, Carl. There's no need to panic.'

She doesn't understand panic, Carl thought. He tried to remember if he had ever seen his mother truly upset. No. He could only think of her sitting placidly with her books or her ridiculous cello. She had never lost anything she cared for.

Nancy Grafton would understand. She remembers her dead child. She would offer to drive me around the town. There would be tension in her features.

'I should start dinner now,' Sara said. 'Why don't you look around the neighborhood ... or at the junk-yard.

Baxter doesn't get there as often now that you're at school.' She went into the kitchen.

Carl walked to the corner where his mother's cello stood. He raised his right leg and kicked his foot out suddenly. The cello snapped in two at the neck, filling the house with the alarming sound of cracking wood and discordantly resonating strings.

As the boy left the house he looked over his shoulder and saw his mother standing in the center of the room, staring at the shattered instrument. She had a look of panic and loss.

Carl slammed the door and headed for the junk-yard.

The afternoon sun cast deep shadows across the jagged piles of wreckage. For the first time the familiar landscape of the yard seemed unappealing to Carl. I've outgrown it, he thought. I won't return to it again.

As he expected, he found the bodies of the puppies uncovered. He looked at them hesitantly, wondering whether he would feel regret. But he felt only the excitement and pride he had felt each time he had thought of them during the day. He couldn't see Baxter, but he knew he was near. He wondered what the dog felt. Fear, he hoped.

The bunker was empty. It seemed small and unpleasant. The boy began to dismantle it, removing supports and climbing on top of it, feeling it collapse beneath his weight. It took only a few minutes to return it to its original, formless state. He sat and rested and wondered why he had been so concerned about Baxter's disappearance. He no longer needed the dog.

The boy got up and started to go back towards town. Then he remembered the pit. He wanted to see it once more. It had been important to him; more important than it had been to the dog.

As he walked Carl felt his perspiration evaporating under the cold wind. And when he saw Baxter standing below in the shadows of the pit he began to shiver. The dog stood motionless; staring; waiting.

'Baxter?'

The dog did not react.

'Baxter! Come!'

Carl watched the dog carefully. Its muscles tightened reflexively, but it did not change its position. I've lost control of him, the boy thought. I'm being challenged. But that was Baxter's mistake; a mistake the dog hadn't made with Mrs. Prescott or the Grafton baby. He had been successful with them because he had used deceit and surprise. But he was presenting an honorable challenge now. It was not always wise to be honorable.

Carl backed away from the pit, looking around for a weapon. He picked up a heavy steel rod and then sat down to consider the situation. It would be dark before long. If Baxter didn't make his move soon, it would be necessary to force him to act. Darkness would give him too much of an advantage.

The boy wondered whether he should enter the pit. No. Even with the proper weapons that would be foolish. But Baxter had to remain in the pit. He would have too much room to maneuver in if he were free. The solution was simple. If the escape stairs were removed the pit would become a grave. The dog could not escape. It could be left to starve, or it could become a target.

Carl got up and went to the area above the boxes that formed the escape steps. He pushed the steel rod between the wall of the pit and the boxes and pried them loose in one quick motion. Baxter dodged the boxes as they fell. He was trapped.

Carl turned away and began to look for something he could throw into the pit; something that would break bones and tear flesh.

3

Jason Fine examined the shattered cello. He had never looked closely at it before. It had been his wife's secret. Now he realized how delicate the instrument was; how deceptive its ungainly size and sturdy sound were. It's like a person, he thought: vulnerable, misleading.

'I think it can be fixed,' he said.

'It doesn't matter,' Sara said.

She seemed remarkably calm to Jason. He hoped she was disguising her feelings. If not—if the incident really didn't matter to her—then Carl had done something unforgivable. He had weakened Sara's ability to care. She couldn't afford that.

'It does matter,' Jason said. 'And I want Carl to understand that. Do you know where he is?'

'At the junk-yard, I suppose. Or wherever the dog is.'

'I'll go get him.'

'Are you going to hurt him?'

'I'm going to try.'

Sara blinked rapidly. She's trying to weep, Jason thought. But she won't; no more than I will. We're not used to being part of a drama. We're trained as spectators: she with her books and I with my gossip. Carl's becoming one of the performers and forcing us to join him. We don't know our lines; our gestures are wrong. We'll punish him for it.

Jason took the cello to the hall closet, put it on the floor among the overshoes, and closed it into the darkness. 'I'll be back soon,' he said.

Sara came to the door with him. 'Don't hurt Carl,' she said. 'He did it because I neglected the dog. He loves the dog.'

As Jason drove through the twilight he wondered whether

people could really love animals. No, he thought. What they love is themselves; a part of themselves they see reflected in the animal. There was nothing admirable about that kind of relationship. It was too one-sided. Jason tried to remember if he had ever heard of a person giving up his or her life to save a dog. No. It didn't work that way.

God help the dog that is loved.

4

There is no way out. I realize now that my life became endangered the first time I entered the circle. The threat was not from my opponents, but from myself. I was performing an act of submission and trust. I submitted myself to the boy's will. I trusted him . . . the way the old woman and the child trusted me.

Trust is the ultimate weakness and a kind of madness. I could only have been insane to think the boy would face me openly in the circle. He knows the importance of deceit and betrayal. It is something he learned from me; something he made me forget.

Strangely, I do not regret my error. It may be inevitable that anyone who lives in the town—even I—must become afflicted with moments of trust. It is something one must accept. I have become vulnerable, but I still have my courage and my physical strength to rely on, and the boy knows that. I have no fear of him.

Yet I am disturbed. What disturbs me is not that I might die, but that I might live. What would become of me in that case? There could be no doubt of my responsibility for the boy's death. Would the people of the town accept me after that? No. I would have to leave them.

Are there other towns? Are there other people living together in uneasy trust, fearing that their trust will fail them as mine has failed me? Could it be that there is a kind of courage in trust? Do the people know that there are those like the boy and me among them? Do they knowingly risk being betrayed by us? They might be more courageous than I thought. I would like to stay among them.

If I could stay, would I seek out another like the boy? Not at first, certainly. I would live quietly with his parents. I would lie in darkened corners, listening to them murmur, wondering what knowledge they were concealing from me.

The boy has returned. He conceals nothing. His malice is obvious, and even now I feel a fleeting admiration for him. We have learned from each other, and something of the other's strength will live on in whichever of us survives.

Strength does not die.

Four

Carl gathered his weapons at the edge of the pit. He had chosen carefully: rocks, scrap metal, objects heavy enough to stun and crush, but not too heavy to be thrown accurately. He was grateful for the sounds the objects made as he stacked them up: harsh, percussive noises that obscured the steady, excited panting of the dog.

First a rock: sharp-edged and dense. As the boy drew back his arm Baxter crouched tensely. The dog sprang easily aside when Carl's arm came forward, and the rock thudded heavily on the cold earth. The boy was not discouraged. He knew the dog's eyesight was not acute. As the sky darkened it would become more difficult to see what was thrown. The dog's whiteness would be visible against the floor of the pit even in complete darkness.

Carl picked up another rock and feinted a throw. Baxter jumped aside. He's reacting to my motion, not to what I'm holding, the boy thought; he can't see the rock. Another feint, followed by a quick second motion and release. The rock missed, but only by a few inches.

As the boy reached for a rusted sash-weight Baxter charged forward and leaped towards the edge of the pit. He came within a foot of the top—closer than the boy had thought possible—but he fell back. It was the dog's maximum effort, Carl thought. It has proved the futility of trying to escape. Another point scored.

And as the dog fell on to its back, scrambling to regain

its footing, Carl quickly threw the sash-weight. It struck Baxter's ribs. No real damage was done; there hadn't been time for the boy to put his full weight behind the throw. But a blow had been landed. Four more attempts; one of them successful. Blood showed on Baxter's left flank, and he began to move more slowly than before.

Carl's supply of rocks had run out. As he looked around for more, his breathing was heavy and uneven. He had forgotten the meaning of what he was doing. He no longer thought in terms of death, but only of completing an action. Baxter was not the animal that had made the summer meaningful, the creature whose presence had been so reassuring and vivid to the boy in his bedroom on sleepless nights. The dog was only a target now; elusive and persistent, but impersonal.

It had become more difficult to find suitable weapons. Carl began to throw whatever met his hands as he groped in the near-darkness. His aim became haphazard, and his strength diminished. It was difficult to tell what effect his attacks were having on Baxter. Carl had not heard the dog whimper or yelp, but he could see dark, glistening patches on its white coat.

The boy wanted it to be over. There must be a better way. He turned away from the pit and reached desperately to the ground. His hand gripped cold, smooth metal. A handle. He was standing on the door of an abandoned refrigerator. That was better. Something large and inescapable. He raised the door. A tombstone, he thought, as he maneuvered it to the edge of the pit. The door balanced on its edge for a moment and then tilted away from the boy, swinging out into the darkness. And he felt himself being pulled with it.

The handle had caught in the cuff of his jacket sleeve. He pulled back desperately, hearing cloth rip, but he was unable to keep his balance. His chest hit the ground, his head and his right arm extending over the space of the pit.

As the door fell Baxter moved clumsily against the pit wall, no longer agile, but still strong enough to shake off the glancing blow of the metal slab. The door lay slightly tilted, forming a shallow-angled ramp. Carl's arm dangled above. The dog moved up the ramp and closed his jaws on the boy's hand, pulling him towards the floor of the pit.

As Carl slid downward he reached out with his free hand, grasping for a hold to stop his fall. He found only the steel rod he had used to pry the stairs loose. He swung the rod wildly as he rolled down the ramp, striking out at Baxter in pain and confusion. In a moment the boy was on his feet, his right hand still gripped by the dog's teeth.

Carl swung the rod again and felt Baxter's hold weaken slightly as the steel struck the dog's spine. But the jaws tightened again immediately. In his pain Carl almost dropped the rod. They stood facing each other, the boy bent forward, trying to ease the pressure in his hand; the dog standing unsteadily; breathing with difficulty.

This is my chance, Carl thought. My last chance, perhaps. Forget your body. Think. The dog is not the master. And then Carl knew what to do. He gripped the rod tightly in his free hand, and he spoke sharply:

'Baxter! Heel!'

For an instant the dog relaxed its grip; just for an instant and only slightly, but it was enough to allow Carl to pull free and raise the rod in both hands. He brought it down powerfully across the dog's neck. Baxter staggered back slightly and then collapsed, his legs twitching. He watched helplessly as the boy lifted the rod again.

2

The pain has stopped, and I no longer feel the cool air against my body. But I know the wind is still strong, for it brings me the sounds and odors of the town with a strange clarity. And as I wait for death, I think not of the boy who stands above me, but of the others, living and dead, whose traces are carried to me.

The odors are varied; differing from one another as much as the people themselves do. The old woman and the child: their scents remain in the dark houses, just as the odors of others cling faintly to the objects that surround us here in the circle. My scent too will remain.

The sounds are distinct but muted. With the changing season, the people have shut themselves behind the windows of their houses. And as the days pass, the quiet will become more complete. Soon the first snow will come and there will be a moment, as the people of the town awaken, when the silence will be absolute. The people will be uneasy, thinking of the silence of death.

Perhaps they will also think of me.

Certainly some of them will.

The boy will.

3

Jason Fine shone the flashlight into the pit.

'Carl,' he shouted.

His son stood with his arms raised above the obviously dead body of Baxter. The boy didn't seem to see the light or hear his name being called. He brought his arms down, striking the dog's battered head.

Jason jumped into the pit. An arena, he thought. A place for death; a man-made place . . . or boy-made. He took the rod from Carl's hands. 'It's over,' he said. 'Are you all right?'

The boy's eyes showed no recognition, but reflected what Jason was afraid might be a kind of pleasure. He turned the light on the dog briefly. There was no need to check for signs of life. No animal could have survived the beating. Did any animal deserve it?

'We'd better bury him,' Jason said.

'He tried to kill me,' Carl said. He held his hand up to the light. Bruise marks stood out against the pale flesh, but the skin was not broken.

'You'll be all right. Let's bury Baxter, then we'll leave.'

'He doesn't deserve it.'

'He's dead, Carl. I'm going to bury him. You can wait in the car if you want to.'

Jason climbed out of the pit to look for something he could use as a shovel. He cast the light beam across the piles of trash and broken objects. He remembered the cello. The boy is comfortable with destruction, he thought. He picked up a dented metal wastebasket and returned to the pit.

Carl watched as his father worked awkwardly to dig the shallow grave. The boy's hand rested on the rod he had used to kill Baxter. He felt pain, and realized his hand was tightening around the weapon. The dog was more important to him than I am, Carl thought. Baxter was a killer, yet he was loved. Why should that be? Maybe because he played the role of dog when it was to his advantage. Subservient, obedient. The boy's hand relaxed. It was not the time to show his resentment. There would be better times; subtler ways.

When the burial was finished Carl went to stand with his father beside the grave. I must show him I can cry, the boy thought. Think of Baxter, he told himself. Remember the battered, pathetic body. But he felt no grief; only a sense of relief and triumph.

He wondered when he had last wept. What had angered or frustrated him that much? Perhaps if he remembered it, he could weep again. But there was nothing to remember. He would have to get along without tears. He picked up the flashlight from the ground where his father had rested it while digging. He shone the light on the loosely packed dirt of the grave.

'I'm sorry, Baxter,' he said.

And he embraced his father. When had he last done that? Maybe at the time he last wept. It was too long ago or too unimportant to recall. I must do it more often, he thought. It's appreciated. 'I'm sorry, Dad.'

Jason held his son tightly. The dog's death had served some purpose after all. Carl had learned something important.

Five

Snow had begun to fall during the night.

Mary Cuzzo awoke uneasily. She was still learning how much she had come to rely on her father's presence in the house. He hadn't been an active or a noisy man, yet for years the small sounds he made as he moved about downstairs in the morning had comforted her. He had always been up before she had, thumping and scraping. The sounds became familiar, but the activities that caused them remained a mystery.

She wondered why this morning's silence seemed deeper than usual. Then she understood: it extended beyond the house. She opened her eyes. There was also something unusual about the quality of the darkness. It was not yet dawn, but the silhouettes of the furniture stood out distinctly against the walls. Was there a full moon?

She went to the window. A thick layer of snow glittered on the sill. Outside the street light glowed with an unusual brightness, casting a brilliant circle at its base. The snow was still falling, tempering the darkness. Now that she stood close to the window, Mary could hear the occasional delicate skittering of flakes against the glass. There was no other sound.

She thought of her father's grave. She would go there today. The last time she visited the cemetery, the mound of still-settling earth had offended her. It had seemed so heavy and oppressive. The grave would look less forbidding under the delicate snow; under the whiteness.

Wasn't white the color of mourning in some countries? That's how it should be everywhere. She thought of how attractive the women always seemed in their black dresses at funerals. White was better: cool and lifeless.

Then the silence was broken by the distant barking of a dog. Mary remembered Carl Fine's white dog. What had become of it? It had been so much a part of the town during the summer. She had envied the uncomplicated affection that the boy and the dog seemed to share. Her father had tried to teach her to dislike dogs as well as affection. He hadn't succeeded. He had taught her only the need to have someone or something dependent on her. Now that she was alone, maybe she could keep a dog.

She tried to imagine what it would be like if a dog were in the room with her now. It would be standing close to her, eager to follow her downstairs to the kitchen. She liked the idea. Where could she get a dog? Carl would know.

2

Queenie barked excitedly as she ran through the yard, breaking a looping path in the fresh snow. Joseph Bartnik watched her from the kitchen window. She's happy, he thought. He knew that since he had taken the puppies from her the dog was happy only when she was away from him. But that didn't matter. What mattered was that she still obeyed him. Happiness was not something that he required either of her or of himself.

The pursuit of happiness. He had never understood how that phrase got into the—what was it?—the Constitution? Life and liberty he understood, but the pursuit of happiness must have been the thought of someone's wife. A man wouldn't have thought it that important. It's women who pursue happiness, and it takes them away from us. He thought of his wife and daughter.

Veronica lay half awake, listening to Queenie's barking. She could hear the gentle clinking of the dog's name tag against its collar. The sound reminded her of something: something unpleasant. Then she remembered. Carl Fine had begun to wear some sort of chain around his neck, and as he sat in class at school he touched it occasionally, producing a soft clinking sound.

Carl would not tell her what had become of the puppies or Baxter. He smiled at her each day and called her Eva. And he walked alone through the streets of the town, looking at curbs and bushes.

Veronica didn't want to share the town with him. She would leave soon: after the first snow, she told herself.

3

The silence will be broken soon, Jason Fine thought. We'll hear the scraping of a shovel against the sidewalk and the whining of tires against packed snow. He went to the bed and touched Sara's shoulder.

'It's snowing,' he said.

Let it please her, he thought. There had been little pleasure for her lately. Carl had embraced her and apologized the night of Baxter's death, but as the boy clung to her she had stared over his shoulder at the wall, her brow wrinkled. Jason couldn't be sure what she had felt, but he knew it wasn't pleasure.

'Sara. Come and see the snow. It's beautiful.'

Sara had not been asleep. She had been grateful when Jason got up and went to the window. He was a noisy sleeper. It frightened her to hear the air being forced through the complicated channels of his nose and throat. She sometimes had to wake him up, afraid that he was choking. It was quiet now. She liked silence. It was the most eloquent part of music: the rests and the pauses that defined the notes.

There was a great deal of silence in her life now. Sometimes in the afternoons she would go to the closet and look at the mutilated cello, but she couldn't bring herself to touch it. It reminded her of Carl, and she tried not to think of him. His new deference and affection were unacceptable to her. It was like having another dog around the house.

She had preferred Baxter.

4

Nancy Grafton was making an angel. She lay on her back, spreading and closing her outstretched legs; pushing her arms in twin arcs through the moist, thick snow. She looked up into the darkness, her mouth open to catch the falling crystals.

She and John had come directly from bed out to their front lawn, pulling on old clothes, and not bothering with breakfast.

She's like a child, John thought, as he stood watching her. A happy child. He tried to remember when her happiness had begun to return. He wasn't sure. Maybe it was when Carl Fine began to appear on the streets without Baxter; when the boy told them the dog was dead.

John reached down and helped Nancy to her feet. They looked at the impression she had made in the snow. An angel. John had never liked the idea of angels. He couldn't believe that death was like that. It frightened him to think that Nancy's body had made the shape that was before them in the darkness. A Dark Angel.

'Now you make one,' Nancy said.

John hesitated. 'Men don't do that.'

'Do it and I'll tell you a secret.'

John lay down in the snow next to his wife's angel. His body recoiled from the damp coldness immediately. For a moment he was motionless, his eyes closed. He thought of graves. Then he moved his arms and legs; quickly, eager to stand again.

When he returned to Nancy she was smiling. And as they looked at the two angels in the snow, she took his hand and said, 'I'd like to have another child.'

EPILOGUE

Carl Fine stood at the bedroom window of the Prescott house. The afternoon sun glinted on the melting snow, throwing into relief the two strange shapes in the Graftons' front yard.

Soon he would hear the couple's automobile approaching. He thought of the night he had stood in their bedroom. He remembered the woman's scent; a subtle, sexually exciting aroma. He had seldom been as happy as at that moment.

He heard the sound of their car approaching. It pulled into the driveway, and for a moment there was life on the block. He could see curtains being pulled aside as neighbors looked resentfully at the couple. The street was soon quiet again. Carl stayed at the window, staring at the couple's house.

What are they doing now? he wondered. He knew what the rooms looked like, and he knew generally how they lived, but that was not enough. He wanted to be there with them. He wanted to be close to them; to go into the bathroom after they had bathed. The steamy air that had touched their bodies would envelop him. He would reach into the hamper and lift out the clothes that were still warm from those bodies.

But he would not be able to do that. Instead he would go to his own home and sit at the dinner table with his tired, commonplace parents. He would eat the carelessly prepared meal, and he would go to his room, leaving them to sit silently before the television set.

Carl stared unblinkingly at the windows of the Graftons'

house. He could see them moving from room to room. He heard their laughter. His parents never laughed any more; they were stolid and dull, the boy thought. I have a strength and knowledge that they have never known. I must use that strength and knowledge.

What would become of me, he wondered, if my parents were to have an accident? What if one night, as they slept, their uninteresting house were to fill with smoke and flames? It could happen quickly ... too quickly to allow escape or rescue. A few neighbors and I would stand helplessly in the cold darkness while ashes formed and mingled. What would become of me if that happened?

The young couple would love me. I'm certain of that. They see the possibility of love everywhere. They saw it in Baxter. They'll see it in me.

CPSIA information can be obtained
at www.ICGtesting.com
Printed in the USA
BVHW030314100123
655977BV00012B/71

9 781954 321830